ID0333764

Portrait of an Outlaw

Scotch John MacGregor has a burning ambition to become as famous an outlaw as his forbear, Rob Roy. And he is well on the way to achieving this aim as he and his gang rampage across the State of Colorado, robbing banks, holding up stagecoaches, and easily eluding the various law enforcement agencies.

However, fate takes a hand when Pinkerton agent, Dave Lansom, meets up with the renowned Kentuckian gunfighter, Jack Stone, and together they combine to track down the outlaws. As Scotch John soon discovers, the pair make a formidable team.

Portrait of an Outlaw

J.D. KINCAID

A Black Horse Western

ROBERT HALE · LONDON

© J.D. Kincaid 2009
First published in Great Britain 2009

ISBN 978-0-7090-8760-1

Robert Hale Limited
Clerkenwell House
Clerkenwell Green
London EC1R 0HT

www.halebooks.com

The right of J.D. Kincaid to be identified as
author of this work has been asserted by him
in accordance with the Copyright, Designs and
Patents Act 1988

Typeset by
Derek Doyle & Associates, Shaw Heath
Printed and bound in Great Britain by
CPI Antony Rowe, Chippenham and Eastbourne

ONE

It was early evening on a mild April day in the year of Our Lord 1885 when John MacGregor eventually reached Colorado Springs. He alighted from the train, dumped his suitcase on the platform and took in a couple of lungfuls of fresh Colorado air. He felt exhilarated and, at the same time, a little apprehensive. Born and bred in Chicago, he had fled that city with $200 of his employer's money in his pocket. Two days earlier, bored with his job as an accounts clerk in a large dry-goods emporium, he had stolen $200 from that day's takings and headed out West. And now here he was, with only the vaguest idea of what he would do next.

Twenty-five years old, John MacGregor was a handsome, red-haired young man of no more than medium height, yet powerfully built. He had a pair of piercing blue eyes and a finely sculpted face, with a straight nose, high cheekbones and a strong jaw. And he cut an imposing figure in his dark grey city-style suit and derby hat. Beneath the jacket he carried a Colt Peacemaker, a gift from his late Uncle Saul.

During his childhood, John MacGregor had spent several summers at his uncle's horse ranch, together with his cousin, Simon Laidlaw, now a junior reporter on the staff of the *Chicago Daily News*. The ranch was situated a few miles outside the small Colorado cattle town of Touchstone and here Uncle Saul had taught the two boys how to shoot, ride, hunt, and break in mustangs. Of the two, John MacGregor had been the more gifted pupil. In particular, he had excelled with the gun.

Upon Uncle Saul's death, the ranch had been sold and his aunt had retired, not to cold and windy Chicago, but to warm and sunny Frisco, where she had subsequently remarried. Nonetheless, when John MacGregor had determined, on the spur of the moment, to make a break and launch out upon a new adventure, he had straightaway chosen to head for the state of Colorado. It was, after all, the only part of the Wild West with which he was at all familiar.

He picked up his suitcase and left the railway station. A quick stroll up and down Colorado Springs' Main Street revealed that, although the town boasted several saloons, it had but the one hotel, the Crystal Queen. Consequently, John MacGregor directed his footsteps towards this establishment.

Once installed in one of the Crystal Queen's bedchambers, a sparsely furnished room which overlooked the stables at the rear of the hotel, MacGregor threw himself down upon the narrow bed and contemplated his future.

As a youth, his imagination had been fired by Sir Walter Scott's 1817 novel, *Rob Roy*. This had been, and still was, a hugely popular work of fiction world-wide. To most Americans it was no more than that, yet its influence upon the young Chicago accounts clerk had been immense, for Rob Roy, too, was a MacGregor, an ancestor. And had not he been Scotland's most famous outlaw, often referred to as the Scotch Robin Hood? Oh that he, John MacGregor, might emulate his renowned forebear! But Rob Roy had had an entire clan at his back, whereas John MacGregor was entirely on his own. So, what to do?

Dissatisfied with the tedium of his life in Chicago, MacGregor had acted upon a sudden impulse. Hence the theft of his employer's money and the flight to Colorado Springs. He had craved a life of adventure and where better to find such a life than in America's Wild West? He could, he supposed, seek a job as a cowboy, perhaps on a cattle drive? That should prove exciting, forging a trail through wild, untamed territory, crossing rivers and mountains and possibly encountering hostile Indians upon the way. It would also be darned hard work.

7

MacGregor decided not to pursue that option for the time being. Another idea had sprung to mind. He had always been a pretty good card-player. Playing poker with friends, he had rarely lost. So that was what he would do, he'd try his luck as a professional gambler.

His immediate future thus decided, MacGregor rose from his bed, slapped on his derby hat at a rakish angle, left the room and hurried downstairs. Now that matters were settled in his mind, he recalled that he had not eaten for some hours. Therefore, he headed straight for the Crystal Queen's restaurant, where he partook of a hearty supper.

Thereafter, he adjourned to the hotel's bar-room, for he felt in need of a drink and, besides, he wanted to check whether there was a game of poker or blackjack in progress.

In the event there wasn't, and MacGregor, weary after his long train journey, resolved against checking to see if there was a game on in any of Colorado Springs' various saloons, at least for that evening. The commencement of his career as a professional gambler could wait a day.

The bar-room was, by the West's standards, pretty sumptuous. It boasted several gilt mirrors and a couple of red-plush settees. All the chairs were similarly covered and the walls were lined with a gold-and-silver patterned wallpaper. Crystal chandeliers replaced the usual brass lamps, and the bar had a splendid marbled top. A stained-glass-panelled door opened into the hotel lobby. John MacGregor was suitably impressed.

He sauntered across the bar-room to the bar and ordered a whiskey. Then he stood, savouring his drink and surveying the scene. Again, by the standards of the West, it was rather sophisticated. The Crystal Queen's bar-room was rarely frequented by either the cowhands from the nearby ranches or the town's riff-raff. Ranch owners, town dignitaries, such as the mayor and his fellow councillors, one or two Army officers from the local fort, and a few well-dressed and evidently prosperous travellers made up its custom. Serving these customers were two experienced and highly competent bartenders, together with a variety of pretty young saloon girls in low-cut, yet elegant and brightly coloured silk and satin gowns. And presiding over these proceedings was Kate Mulligan.

Kate Mulligan was an attractive black-haired woman in her early thirties. Warm, inviting brown eyes and a wide, sensuous mouth gave her face an undeniably voluptuous look, while her *décolleté* scarlet-silk gown showed off to advantage her slender figure and firm white breasts. She sidled up to the newcomer.

'Howdy, stranger,' she said. 'Welcome to the Crystal Queen.'

'Thank you, Miss . . . er. . . ?'

'Mulligan, but most folks call me Kate.'

'Wa'al, Kate, my name's John MacGregor. I take it that you're the proprietress of this here hotel?'

'Nope. The hotel's owned by Jake Sellers. My intended.'

MacGregor grinned.

'An' jest where is your intended this evenin', Kate?' he enquired.

'Oh, he has some business he needs to conduct in Denver. I'm expectin' him back sometime tomorrow.'

'Indeed?'

Yeah. So, what brings you to Colorado Springs, Mr MacGregor? Are you some kinda salesman?'

'Nope. I'm a gamblin' man.'

'Wa'al, if it's a game of poker you're lookin' for—'

'Not tonight.'

'You got somethin' else in mind?' Kate smiled and indicated the saloon girls with a wave of her hand. 'My gals are mighty accomodatin'. Take your pick,' she said.

MacGregor ran his eye appraisingly over the bevy of beauties, most of whom seemed already to have attached themselves to one or other of the hotel's male customers.

'You fancy anyone in partickler?' asked Kate.

'I sure do!' said MacGregor enthusiastically.

'Which one?'

He looked her straight in the eye.

10

'I've kinda taken a fancy to you, Kate,' he said.

Kate laughed and replied, 'I told you, Mr MacGregor, I'm what you might call engaged. To Jake Sellers.'

'Who ain't here right now.'

'You suggestin' I cheat on him?'

'You got it in one.'

'But—'

'You cain't be sure he ain't cheatin' on you. There are probably some darned pretty gals in Denver, an' jest as accomodatin' as your young ladies here.'

'Jake wouldn't—'

'No?'

Kate considered the matter. Jake probably would. He was often away on business, mostly transacting land and property deals. And she had sometimes wondered whether he might be mixing business with pleasure. Also, although they had been together for almost three years, and despite her frequent hints, he had not so far offered to marry her.

Kate was tempted. The young stranger was both handsome and powerfully built, quite unlike Jake Sellers, who was no oil painting and downright skinny.

'Take your hat off,' she said.

MacGregor obliged and Kate stood for a few moments, admiring his head of thick red hair.

'I ain't never been to bed with a red-headed

man,' she declared.

'There's always gotta be a first time.'

'I s'pose.'

'You said your intended is due back tomorrow and, 'sides, I could be gone by then.'

Kate smiled seductively.

'It'll cost you,' she said. 'I don't come cheap.'

'I figure you'll be worth it, whatever you charge,' replied MacGregor, grinning broadly.

'OK. Let's go upstairs.'

MacGregor threw back the remains of his whiskey, then linked arms with Kate and the pair strolled out of the bar-room and into the hotel lobby.

The financial transaction was conducted swiftly and amicably in John MacGregor's bedchamber, whereupon they hurriedly stripped off their clothes and leapt into bed together.

It was some considerable time since MacGregor had enjoyed a woman's favours and he threw himself upon the girl with glee. Kate, for her part, responded wholeheartedly. Their passions inflamed, they embarked upon a prolonged bout of riotous, uninhibited lovemaking. Indeed, they barely paused for breath during the two hours they were together and their congress might have continued unabated throughout the night, had they not been interrupted.

The interruption, when it came, was both sudden and unexpected. The door of the bedroom was flung open and a rake-thin individual, sporting a black Prince Albert coat and low-crowned, wide-brimmed Stetson, burst in upon them. They immediately sprang apart, Kate Mulligan exclaiming, 'My God, Jake!'

Jake Sellers, for it was he, stood glaring down at them, his dark eyes glinting malevolently.

'You li'l tramp!' he rasped.

'I . . . I didn't expect you back from Denver until tomorrow,' gasped the girl.

'Finished my business earlier than I reckoned.' Jake Sellers' gaunt features were contorted into a furious scowl as he hissed, 'I don't take kindly to bein' cuckolded.'

'But how . . . how did you know I was up here, in this room?'

'I asked where you were. Gus told me 'bout you leavin' the bar-room with that thar feller, an' Jerry gave me his room number.'

Kate nodded glumly. One of the bartenders and the hotel clerk had, between them, betrayed her.

'Look here, Jake—' she began.

'Shuddup!' The hotel owner turned his gaze upon John MacGregor. He flicked back his Prince Albert coat to reveal a pearl-handled .45 calibre British Tranter in the holster on his right hip. He dropped his hand on to the butt. 'You're dead, feller,' he informed the young red-headed man from Chicago.

But he was wrong.

MacGregor promptly threw himself off the bed and on to the floor. Beside him lay his hastily discarded clothes. They formed an untidy pile, on the top of which lay his derby hat and his gun-belt, holster and Colt Peacemaker. MacGregor snatched the gun from its holster, rolled over, aimed and fired, all in one quick, continuous movement. This was done so fast that the first bullet struck Jake Sellers in the chest before he could even raise his British Tranter. The gun was only just clear of its holster when the force of the shot sent him reeling backwards, to collide with the doorpost. A second shot blasted him out through the open doorway into the narrow corridor beyond. Sellers hit the far wall and slid to the floor. He landed with a dull thud and lay quite still.

Kate leapt naked from the bed and ran out to where Sellers lay. She crouched down beside him. She had never truly loved him, yet they had been together for some considerable time and he was her bread and butter. What would happen to her now? She knew that he had a nephew who, in all likelihood, would inherit the hotel and could, if he so wished, kick her out. She turned to confront MacGregor, her face chalk-white and her eyes wild.

'You . . . you've killed him!' she screamed.

MacGregor, meantime, was hastily donning his clothes.

'Of course I killed him,' he snarled. 'If I hadn't, he would sure as hell have killed me.'

He strapped on his gun, placed his hat upon his head and hefted his suitcase, and stepped through the doorway. He skirted both the girl and the body of the late hotel owner and hurried off down the corridor. Her screams followed him as he clattered downstairs and into the hotel lobby.

This was now filled with several of the hotel's customers and sporting women. The sound of the shots had brought them bustling out of the barroom. One of the bartenders was also present and he was clutching a shotgun. As MacGregor hurtled down the stairs, the bartender raised the gun. But he was too late. MacGregor aimed and fired a third time, and blew the bartender's brains out through the back of his skull. The bartender crashed to the floor and the others rushed, in a panic-stricken surge, back into the bar-room. None of them wanted to be John MacGregor's next victim.

That fate was reserved for Marshal Bill Jones. Colorado Springs' veteran lawman, a tall, rangy grey-haired sixty-year-old, had just stepped out of the law office across the street when the first of the shots rang out. He had paused, not quite sure from whence it came. He could scarcely believe that it had come from the Crystal Queen, since, unlike the town's various saloons, it had a reputation for respectability. After some moments' deliberation, the marshal stepped down off the sidewalk and slowly ambled across the street in the direction of the hotel. He was clambering up the flight of wooden steps on to the stoop outside the Crystal Queen when John MacGregor loosed off his third shot. This time there could be no mistake. The shot had quite definitely come from inside the hotel.

Marshal Bill Jones crossed the stoop and flung open the hotel's front door. Sprawled out on the lobby floor before him was the dead bartender, blood and brains oozing from his skull. Facing him was John MacGregor, still clutching his Colt Peacemaker. Bill Jones made a grab for his gun and, in the same instant, MacGregor fired. The .45-calibre bullet struck the marshal in the chest and penetrated his heart. He staggered backwards across the stoop, to tumble head over heels down the wooden steps to the street below.

It was at this point that MacGregor decided to abandon his suitcase. He needed to lam out of town post-haste and, if that meant discarding a few clothes, so be it. He dropped the suitcase on to the lobby floor and sprinted outside.

There were few people abroad in Main Street. Most of Colorado Springs' citizens were either at home or frequenting its saloons. The shots had brought some of them out on to the street, but not many. And the sight of MacGregor, emerging from the hotel gun in hand, was enough to make those few retreat into the shadows.

Yellow light spilled out of the hotel's windows and illuminated the hitching rail in front of its entrance. MacGregor observed that there were a number of horses tied to this rail, no doubt belonging to some of the Crystal Queen's customers. He chose what seemed to him to be the pick of the bunch, namely a splendid coal-black mare. He unhitched her, then leapt into the saddle. Although it was some years since he had mounted a horse, he had not lost the knack. He slipped the Colt Peacemaker back into its holster, turned the mare's head and galloped off down Main Street in the direction of the open prairie beyond.

Behind him, three of the hotel's customers emerged cautiously into the lobby. They wore grey Stetsons and long, ankle-length brown-leather coats and, like MacGregor, were strangers in town. The tallest of the three had a harsh, pockmarked countenance and lank brown hair hanging down to his shoulders, and he walked with a pronounced limp. His companions were short, stocky men, both heavily bearded. All three had looked a little out of place in the Crystal Queen's bar-room. They had ventured in only because they were ravenously hungry at the end of a long day's ride and the aroma of food wafting out of the hotel kitchen had tempted them into its restaurant. After the meal, they had drifted into the bar-room and had been contemplating leaving its smart, fashionable interior for the rather more rough and ready atmosphere of one of the town's saloons when the shooting began.

17

Now they hurried outside in the wake of John MacGregor. They reached the stoop just as he rode off.

'That's the kinda feller we need to take Lyle's place,' asserted the one with the limp.

'You reckon?' growled the older of his two companions.

'I do.'

'Then let's git after him,' said the third man.

Without more ado, the three mounted their horses, which earlier they had hitched to the rail outside the hotel. They dug their spurs into their mounts' flanks and set off in the direction taken by their unsuspecting quarry.

A clear starlit sky enabled John MacGregor's pursuers to follow him without difficulty as he rode across the prairie towards the distant mountains. It also enabled him to detect that he was being pursued, and by how many riders. He cursed beneath his breath and increased his speed, heading for the nearest foothills.

Upon reaching them, MacGregor promptly galloped up the narrow, winding trail ahead of him, This would have taken him past a stand of cottonwoods had he not chosen to ride into the shadow of these trees. Once there, he drew the Colt Peacemaker from his holster and quickly reloaded it. And waited.

'Hold hard and raise your goddam hands!'

This command barked at them out of the dark-

18

ness caused his three pursuers to rein in their horses and slowly stick their hands in the air.

'Where the hell are you?' demanded the one with the limp.

'Never mind where I am. I can see you three quite clearly. So, don't try no tricks.'

'We don't intend to.'

'No? You'll be sayin' next you ain't lookin' to catch me an' claim a reward.'

'What reward? Hell, there ain't been time for one to git posted!'

'That's right. We ain't no bounty hunters,' added the older of the bearded pair.

'Then what in tarnation are you? Some kinda posse?' rasped MacGregor.

'Nope. Let me introduce myself. I'm Bart Harris, though everyone calls me Limpy. An' these two are the Duff brothers, Dan an' Nick. Dan's the elder.'

'So?'

'We rode with Lyle Cochrane.'

'Look, I'm new to these parts. That name means nuthin' to me,' said MacGregor.

'We was his gang. Ol' Lyle, he was 'bout the most famous outlaw hereabouts.'

'Was?'

'Yeah. He got hisself shot dead a coupla months back, durin' a bank robbery that went wrong.'

'Since then we've jest kinda drifted aimlessly,' said Dan Duff.

19

'That's right. We ain't no good on our own. We need a leader,' explained his brother.

'Which is why we came a-chasin' you,' stated Limpy Harris.

'Oh, yeah?'

'Yeah. We . . . er . . . liked your style; the way you gunned down the bartender an' the marshal. That was some fancy shootin',' declared Harris.

'Shootin' which placed you on the wrong side of the law,' stated Dan Duff.

'So, you might as well throw in your lot with us,' remarked Nick Duff.

'As our leader,' said Harris.

John MacGregor carefully considered the three outlaws' proposal. And the more he thought about it, the better he liked the idea. It appealed to his vanity. He had thrown up his old life as a mere clerk in Chicago, to do what? Simply to become one of the hundreds of professional gamblers who roamed the West? That *had* been his plan. But now he had the opportunity to make a name for himself. Was not his ancestor, Rob Roy MacGregor, Scotland's most famous outlaw? Therefore, why should not he, John MacGregor, become the most famous outlaw in the whole of the USA? He thought long and hard. Rob Roy's fame had spread world-wide thanks to Sir Walter Scott's best-selling novel. What he needed was someone to bring his future exploits to the notice of the general public. John MacGregor smiled. He knew just the man.

'OK, boys,' he said. 'You reckoned your boss, Lyle Cochrane, was pretty darned famous. Wa'al, I figure I'm gonna make us the most famous an' successful gang of outlaws in the entire West.'

'That's fine by me,' said Limpy Harris.

'An' by us,' added Dan Duff, speaking for both himself and his younger brother.

'Yeah, John MacGregor . . . no . . . *Scotch* John MacGregor an' his gang are about to be unleashed upon the unsuspectin' state of Colorado.' The red-haired young outlaw grinned. The name, Scotch John MacGregor, had a certain ring to it that greatly appealed to him. 'OK, Limpy, Dan, Nick, you ride with me.'

'So, what do we call you?' enquired Limpy Harris. 'Scotch John, I guess?'

'Nope. You call me boss,' said Scotch John.

'OK, boss, what now?' growled Dan Duff.

Scotch John cogitated for a few moments. Then he recalled a certain log cabin, where, during his childhood holidays, his uncle had taken him and his cousin Simon on hunting expeditions. It was hidden deep in the mountains, in a remote box canyon. The perfect place to hide out while he planned the gang's first exploit.

'We head up into the mountains an' lie low for a few days,' he said. 'Let things quieten down 'fore I lead you fellers on our first raid.'

The others mumbled their agreement to this

21

proposal, whereupon Scotch John rode out from amongst the trees. He headed off through the foothills towards the mountains. Limpy Harris and the Duff brothers followed.

TWO

It was high noon, one week after Jake Sellers' sudden death and those of the marshal and the bartender. A price had been placed upon the head of their killer, although his identity remained unknown. These killings remained the focus of talk and speculation in all the towns surrounding Colorado Springs. One such town was the small cattle township of Cripple Creek, halfway between the Springs and Touchstone. And it was into this sleepy, dusty township that the stagecoach clattered on that sun-drenched April day.

Few people disembarked. There were three in all: a red-faced, portly whiskey salesman in a loud check suit and light-grey derby hat, a black-clad, top-hatted, whey-faced clergyman, arrived to conduct a funeral, and a slim, young man in a neat brown city-style suit and derby hat to match. The last-mentioned had short, corn-coloured hair, a pair of innocent blue eyes and an honest, open countenance. And he peered about him through a pair of wire-framed spectacles.

He carried his two carpetbags from the stage-coach, up a short flight of wooden steps and on to the sidewalk in front of Tanner's Hotel. Then, after pausing for breath, he headed straight into the hotel.

From his bedroom window in this same hotel, Scotch John MacGregor watched the young man enter. He smiled, crossed the room and opened his bedroom door a few inches. He waited until eventually, having signed in at the reception desk downstairs, the newcomer appeared in the upstairs corridor, where he proceeded to open the door of the bedchamber which he had been allocated. It was at this juncture that Scotch John stepped out into the corridor and addressed him.

'Good day, cousin, I trust your journey wasn't too tedious?'

The other started, then smiled nervously.

'Oh, h-hullo, John! I . . . I thought this might be from you,' he stammered, producing from his jacket pocket the telegram which had brought him to Cripple Creek. Scotch John grinned and followed his cousin into the latter's bedchamber. He took the telegram from his cousin's hand and read it aloud: *'Be at Tanner's Hotel in Cripple Creek, Colorado, by noon on Wednesday. I shall contact you there. Big story about to break. Rob Roy.* Succinct and to the point I'd say.'

24

'Yes,' said Simon Laidlaw, adding, 'When we were young, we often talked about our famous Scotch forebear. Therefore, I guessed at once that you had sent the wire.' As an ambitious junior reporter, working on the staff of the *Chicago Daily News*, he had naturally responded to the other's invitation.

Scotch John quietly shut the bedroom door and planted himself on the only chair in the room. Simon Laidlaw, meantime, sat down on the edge of the bed.

'So, what's this all about? What is this big story that's about to break?' enquired Laidlaw.

'It's quite simple,' said Scotch John. 'I want to be as famous as our ancestor, Rob Roy.'

'But ... but he was an outlaw! Surely you don't—?'

'Oh, yes I do!'

'Look, John, I know you stole that money from your employer and fled from Chicago, yet that was a relatively minor crime. For God's sake don't commit a worse one! If you're considering robbing a bank or—'

'I shot three fellers back in Colorado Springs,' Scotch John interrupted him.

'You did what?'

'Let me explain.' Scotch John proceeded to relate to his cousin all that had occurred in Colorado Springs. And he concluded by saying, 'I'm a wanted man now, so what the hell! I ain't got nuthin' to lose. 'Sides, I've got me a small band of outlaws, who elected me their leader. They followed me when I lammed outa town. I thought they were aimin' to take me in, but, no, they were lookin' for a new leader, their old boss havin' recently got hisself killed.'

'You take this on and you'll get *yourself* killed!' cried Laidlaw.

'That's a chance I'm prepared to take.'

'But . . . but where do I come in? Why send for me?'

' 'Cause, like I said, I've got me a cravin' to be somebody famous. I guess it's in my blood. Rob Roy—'

'Is dead and buried. And I don't believe he set out looking for fame. He was forced into outlawry.'

'Wa'al, that's as maybe. The point is, you're a newspaperman an' I want you to report my exploits. You can wire your reports to the *Chicago Daily News* an' arrange for these stories to be syndicated throughout the States. I'd like 'em to appear in all the biggies: the *New York Times*, the *Washington Post*, the *Denver News*, the. . . .'

'OK! OK! I've got the picture.'

'You'd be makin' a name for yourself at the same time. The hot-shot reporter,' said Scotch John.

Laidlaw perked up at this remark. He was at present a very junior reporter and looked likely to remain so. He was only too aware that, so far, he had by no means impressed his editor with his journalistic skills. But his cousin was right. In a very short time, he could become one of the *Chicago Daily News*' ace reporters. And he would make sure that he got a cut of the syndication fees. He suddenly began to view Scotch John's descent into a life of crime in a whole new light.

'OK,' he said. 'I'll do it.'

'*Scotch* John MacGregor. That's what you'll call me,' said the outlaw.

'Hmm, yes. I like that,' admitted Laidlaw. 'A good name for an outlaw.'

'That's what I thought.'

'I shall keep a record of every report I file.'

'Oh, yeah?'

'Yes, for I propose, in due course, to produce a book describing all of your exploits.'

'A biography, you mean?'

'Exactly.'

Scotch John smiled delightedly.

'When I've made my fortune, I shall retire, assume a new identity an' enjoy the good life in mebbe New York or Boston, or even abroad some place,' he declared.

'If you aren't hanged first,' said his cousin, with a wry grin.

The outlaw laughed.

'The authorities gotta catch me first,' he said. 'An' that won't be easy. After each robbery, I aim to vanish into the mountains. Tryin' to find me there will be like lookin' for a needle in a haystack.'

'So, that's why you chose to flee to Colorado, because you can remember the territory from our childhood vacations. Where are you figuring on hiding out? Some place near Uncle Saul's old horse ranch just outside Touchstone?'

'You got it'

'Not his hunting lodge?'

'Mebbe.'

'Could you find it after all these years? As I recall, it was hidden away deep in the heart of the mountains.'

'We went there often enough. I can find it, but you're right about its remoteness. I don't reckon nobody else is likely to stumble across it.'

'No.'

'Could *you* find it?'

The young reporter scratched his head and reflected upon this question for some moments. His mind went back to those halcyon summers he had spent there.

'Yes, I reckon I could,' he said at last.

'Wa'al, keep that information to yourself,' rasped Scotch John.

'I will, cousin, believe me,' promised Laidlaw.

'By the way, how did you git your editor to agree to your leavin' Chicago an' headin' way down here to Cripple Creek,' enquired Scotch John curiously.

'That's easy,' replied Laidlaw. 'I showed him

your telegram and requested that I be allowed to follow up the promised story.'

'An' he agreed jest like that?'

'Yes. He did.'

'Did he, by any chance, guess that I was in fact the mysterious sender, Rob Roy?'

'No, he did not.'

'The report of my crime an' subsequent disappearance must've featured in the pages of the *Chicago Daily News*?'

'Yes, but it was scarcely front-page news, and, anyway, nobody on the newspaper knew of my connection with you. I'm not particularly close to any of my colleagues, you see.'

'So, the editor is unaware that we are cousins?'

'Yes. Quite unaware. And as the story of you absconding with two hundred dollars of your employer's takings quickly became old news and was just as quickly forgotten, he had no reason to connect it with the wire which I received.'

'Good!'

'So, what happens next, John?'

'My gang ride into town 'bout mid-afternoon.'

'Today?'

'Yeah, today. I'm s'posed to rendezvous with 'em jest outside town in' – and here Scotch John consulted his fob-watch – 'one hour's time. Then we ride into town an' rob the bank. You will witness the raid from your bedroom window an' then wire a report to your newspaper.' The outlaw grinned

29

and added, 'The bank's across the street, exactly opposite the hotel.'

'How convenient,' commented Simon Laidlaw.

'Ain't it? An' afterwards you will return to Chicago an' fix up a deal regardin' the syndication of this an' all future stories.'

'And just how do I explain my foreknowledge of these exploits?'

'You have an informant, whose identity you must at all costs protect. That surely ain't so very unusual in the newspaper business, is it?'

'No, it's not,' concurred Laidlaw.

'So, d'you reckon that your editor will agree to this li'l plan?'

'I do.'

'Fine! Wa'al, I'll be sure to wire you, informin' you when an' where we aim to strike next. 'Course I'll word it so as to disguise its meanin' from anyone, other than yourself, who might chance to read it. An' I'll sign it "Rob Roy" as before.'

'And you'll send it where?'

'To the *Chicago Daily News* offices, also as before.'

'No, you won't.'

'Why not?'

'Because I don't intend spending most of my time over the next few months travelling between Chicago and the state of Colorado. I want to be situated somewhere in Colorado, so that I can reach the scene of each of your exploits quickly and without too much trouble.'

Scotch John nodded. His cousin's point was a valid one.

'Hmm,' he said, 'that makes good sense. OK, I suggest you make your headquarters in Colorado Springs. That's pretty central. Take a room at the Crystal Queen Hotel. I'll contact you there. But, jest one thing, how will you explain your various absences?'

Simon Laidlaw smiled silkily.

'I shall tell them at the hotel that I am a historian engaged in writing a history of the state of Colorado, and that my researches will take me out of town from time to time.'

'Yeah, that should do it, Simon. The perfect cover,' remarked Scotch John.

'However, you'll be sending me wires to the same telegraph office each time. OK, so you keep them pretty innocent-sounding and sign them "Rob Roy". But it's possible the telegraphist might eventually put two and two together.'

'Yeah, he might. Eventually.' Scotch John grinned. 'These wires will be sent several days *before* each robbery and several weeks'll elapse between each robbery. I figure it'll be some time, if ever, before the telegraphist guesses that "Rob Roy" is a pseudonym for Scotch John MacGregor.'

'Yes. But what do we do then?'

'Mebbe I'll have accumulated enough loot for me to retire 'fore he figures it out. Hell, it's a chance I'm prepared to take!'

Yes, thought Laidlaw. *You really do want to be as famous as your forebear.* Aloud, he said, 'OK, John, it's your neck that's on the line. Let's give it a go.'

Scotch John nodded and rose to his feet.

'Wa'al, I'd best be goin',' he remarked. 'I don't wanta be late.'

The two cousins thereupon shook hands and Scotch John MacGregor turned to leave.

'Good luck!' cried Laidlaw.

The outlaw smiled and was gone.

Laidlaw continued to sit on the edge of the bed. His mind was in a turmoil. Could his cousin pull off robbery after robbery and still evade capture, he asked himself? If he could, then his, Laidlaw's, future was secured. He would progress from junior to ace reporter; his salary, he reckoned, would double; and, besides, there would be his share of the syndication monies to come. Also, after his cousin eventually laid aside his gun, Laidlaw would have a potentially best-selling biography to offer to the publishing world. Everything depended upon the success or otherwise of Scotch John MacGregor and his gang. Laidlaw sighed. Ought he to head for Cripple Creek law office and tell the town marshal all that he knew? Or should he take a chance and go along with his cousin's plan? To do so would make him an accessory before the fact. Oh, what the hell! This was his big chance and he determined to grab it.

Meantime, while Laidlaw was still contemplating

his future, Scotch John was riding west out of Cripple Creek. He followed the main trail for a couple of miles and then branched off into and along a narrow gully. A few hundred yards down this gully, three men were crouched round a camp-fire, smoking cheroots and drinking coffee. They glanced up as Scotch John approached.

'Wa'al, boss, is it all set?' enquired Limpy Harris eagerly.

The two Duff brothers eyed their new leader and prayed that he would prove luckier than the late lamented Lyle Cochrane.

'It is,' said Scotch John. 'I've reconnoitred Cripple Creek pretty darned thoroughly an' I reckon this, our first raid, oughta be a piece of cake.'

'Oh, yeah?' said Dan Duff.

'Yeah. The law office is situated halfway between the bank an' the town's eastern limits. So, if we ride into town from here, we don't have to pass the law office. We hold up the bank an' are outa there 'fore the marshal an' his deppities know what's what.'

'Sounds easy,' remarked Nick Duff.

'It will be,' said Scotch John, 'providin' we all do as I say.'

'OK, boss, tell us what we've gotta do,' growled Limpy Harris.

'We all four ride into town nice an' easy, an' hitch up to the rail outside Tanner's Hotel. This stands directly opposite the Cattlemen's Bank. You, Limpy, will remain there with the horses, while me an' the others cut across the street an' enter the bank. You'll act as look-out an', if the need arises, lead our horses across Main Street to the bank. Is that clear?'

'Yup.'

'What about us?' enquired Dan Duff.

'You two will make sure the teller an' everyone else in the bank keeps their hands in the air an' their mouths shut. I'll git the manager to open the safe an' fill as many money sacks as are needed to hold the bank's funds. Then, we dash back across to where Limpy is holdin' our horses an' high-tail it outa town.' Scotch John glanced at each of his accomplices in turn. 'Any questions?' he demanded.

All three shook their heads. Scotch John grinned broadly.

'Then let's go,' he said.

Limpy Harris kicked dirt on to the fire to extinguish it, the coffee pot and mugs were stashed away, and the three outlaws quickly mounted and followed their young, red-headed leader out of the gully and on to the trail. They turned right and headed off towards Cripple Creek.

When they reached the town the four riders found Main Street pretty much deserted. Most of the stores were shut, for it was the time when Cripple Creek's citizens were taking a nap after lunch. The feed-and-grain store, the stage-line depot and the Cattlemen's Bank were about the only establishments remaining open.

The four dismounted outside Tanner's Hotel as planned and hitched their horses to the rail. Limpy Harris promptly made pretend he was examining each horse in turn, in an effort to prevent anyone from suspecting he was up to no good. Meanwhile, the other three strolled nonchalantly across the street towards the bank.

As they entered the bank all three pulled their kerchiefs up to cover their faces and drew their guns. Scotch John drew his Colt Peacemaker, while the Duff brothers drew their Remington revolvers.

'This is a stick-up!' yelled Scotch John. 'Keep your mouths shut, an' don't none of you try to be a hero, an' nobody'll git hurt.'

'Yeah. Put your hands in the air, all of you,' added Dan Duff menacingly.

There were two bank employees: a thin, nervous-looking, grey-haired man, whom Scotch John took to be the manager, and a pimply-faced youth. As for customers, there were only three present: an elderly widow, who owned the town's dry-goods store; the manager of Tanner's Hotel; and a young man in cowboy's attire, the son of a rancher whose spread was situated a mile or so outside Cripple Creek. All of them, bank employees and customers alike, quickly obeyed Scotch John's and Dan Duff's instructions.

'OK,' snarled Scotch John, addressing the grey-haired bank manager. 'Now, open the safe. An' remember, no tricks.'

He lifted a wooden flap, stepped behind the counter and prodded the reluctant manager with his revolver. Pale-faced, perspiring and trembling, the man led the way into a back office, in the corner of which stood a large iron safe. Then, without further ado, he produced a set of keys and proceeded to unlock the safe. He threw open the door to reveal several shelves stacked with banknotes of different denominations. Also inside was a quantity of money sacks. Scotch John gestured towards these sacks.

'Fill them sacks!' he rasped.

'But—'

'Fill 'em!'

The bank manager made no further protest, but immediately set to stuffing the various banknotes into the sacks. By the time he had filled three and partly filled a fourth, the safe was empty.

'OK. Fill up that last sack with what you've got in them tills behind the counter,' said Scotch John.

The bank manager, still shaking like a leaf, hastily complied. Then, when the last banknote was safely thrust inside that fourth sack, Scotch John turned to Nick Duff.

'Come through here an' give me a hand. There's four sacks. We'll carry two each.'

'OK, boss.'

Nick Duff dropped his Remington back into its holster and hurried through the gap where the flap had been. He picked up two of the sacks. At the same time, Scotch John returned his gun to its holster and lifted the other two sacks. Then they dashed back through to the opposite side of the counter and headed for the door.

It was at this point that the rancher's son summoned up sufficient courage to make his move. He pulled out his revolver and fired at Dan Duff. But he was no marksman and his shot was hurried. Consequently it missed its target, whistling past the outlaw's left ear and burying itself in the bank's doorframe. Dan Duff straightaway responded. The outlaw's .45-calibre slug struck the young man in the right shoulder, knocking him clean off his feet. He hit the floor, the widow screamed, the bank manager fainted and the teller dropped out of sight behind the counter.

'Holy cow!' cried Scotch John. 'Let's git the hell outa here!'

The three fled out of the door to find Main Street no longer deserted. The shots had alerted Cripple Creek's citizens. Among those who had erupted into Main Street were Deputy Hal Robbins and Leo Brandon, proprietor of the town's general store. Unlike the town marshal, who had emerged from the law office, his deputy, having just visited the general store, stood between Scotch John and his gang and their line of escape. He and the storekeeper stood shoulder to shoulder in the middle of Main Street, he brandishing his Colt Peacemaker and Leo Brandon clutching a shotgun.

Brandon fired first and missed. The outlaws promptly responded and, in so doing while at the same time mounting their horses, they dropped two of the money sacks. Scotch John swore, but realized that, should he dismount to retrieve them, he would in all likelihood be either gunned down or captured.

Cutting his losses, he dug his heels into his horse's flanks and galloped straight towards the deputy and the storekeeper. His three confederates did likewise and all four emptied their revolvers into the two unfortunate yet courageous townsmen.

Deputy Hal Robbins was hit twice in the chest and once in the throat. He went down with blood spurting up out of his jugular. He landed on his back in the dust and lay there, his life-blood ebbing away. By the time the outlaws had cleared the town limits he was already dead.

As for Leo Brandon, he was luckier. He was hit twice, but neither shot proved fatal. The first went straight through the fleshy part of his right thigh. The second broke his collarbone, spun him round and sent him sprawling face downwards on to the ground.

The marshal and various other citizens fired

their weapons at the fast-departing outlaws, but with no chance of hitting them, for by this time Scotch John and his gang were well out of range.

In the immediate aftermath of the bank robbery the marshal hastily gathered together a posse to pursue the robbers, the town's doctor attended to the wounded storekeeper, the mortician removed Deputy Hal Robbins' corpse to the funeral parlour, the mayor and several members of the town council gathered outside the bank and discussed the incident at considerable length, and Simon Laidlaw, who had witnessed everything from his hotel window, busily drafted his report.

And, within half an hour of Scotch John and his gang quitting Cripple Creek, the young newspaperman had found his way to the telegraph office and wired his first dispatch to the *Chicago Daily News*.

THREE

Two weeks after the bank robbery at Cripple Creek, the Overland stagecoach was travelling through Colorado on its way from Denver to Pueblo. It was mid-afternoon on a hot, sunny May day and the stage's next port of call was the small mining town of High Cactus.

Driving the stagecoach was veteran driver Joe Bradley, a craggy-faced Texan. Curly grey-speckled hair peeped out from beneath his wide-brimmed grey Stetson, faded blue eyes peered watchfully at the trail ahead, stubble covered his cheeks and jaw and he chewed continuously on a wad of tobacco. A red kerchief, check shirt, brown leather vest, work-worn Levis and a pair of dusty, down-at-heel boots completed his attire.

Sitting up on the box beside Joe Bradley was his shotgun guard, a youngster named Mickey Price. He was attired similarly, although his hat was a smart black low-crowned Stetson and his boots were neither dusty nor down-at-heel. Mickey Price was new to the job and ready for action. He had headed West looking for adventure and, so far, had found little if any. Two years as a ranch hand had proved to be darned hard work and provided precious little excitement. Now he was hoping that his job as a shotgun guard would provide the thrills he craved. Just let someone try to hold up this stagecoach, he thought!

His passengers had no such wish. All they wanted was a quick and peaceful journey, unimpeded by any incident. There were five of them inside the coach, four headed for High Cactus and the fifth intending to continue on to Pueblo.

The four had been visiting the state capital, Denver, in order to attend a state function. They consisted of two couples and had been invited to this function since the men were respectively mayor and deputy mayor of High Cactus.

Horace Potterton, the mayor, was a large, portly man, somewhat flamboyantly dressed in a tall stovepipe hat and black Prince Albert coat, beneath which he wore a sparkling white shirt with a ruffled collar and a crimson brocade vest, which stretched tightly over his enormous girth. A neat crimson tie, sharply creased black trousers and highly polished black shoes completed the picture. His wife, Nancy, was equally expensively attired in a splendid sky-blue-silk gown and matching satin cape, neither of which did anything to disguise her stoutness. A feathery creation perched precariously on top of her mass of blonde curls.

The other couple were rather less ostentatiously dressed. Sidney Squill, the deputy mayor, wore a grey city-style suit and derby hat and his vest matched the colour of the jacket. He was a small, insignificant-looking man, with solemn grey eyes and a pale, thin face which boasted a thin, mousey moustache. His wife, Dorothy, although clad in silks, had chosen bottle-green, and her straw hat, while stylish, was tastefully so. Like her husband, she was not someone who would stand out in a crowd.

The fifth passenger was heading for Pueblo on business. An East-coast land agent, he was hoping to extend his company's dealings to take in Colorado. Other company representatives were similarly travelling out West to other states for the same purpose. Harry Laine, for that was his name, was a slim, elegant-looking man in his mid-thirties. Shrewd brown eyes looked out of a handsome, clean-cut face. He wore a smart brown Stetson and a neat brown city-style suit, and he was a young man keen and ambitious to make a name for himself in his chosen profession.

Silence reigned inside the stagecoach. The passengers had run out of conversation and four of them were expecting soon to arrive at their destination. The coach had slowed its pace considerably, for the last three miles leading up to High

Cactus comprised a long, winding incline through hilly terrain. Also, the horses were beginning to tire. Joe Bradley urged them on, anxious to reach the town and partake of some beer and victuals while the change of horses was accomplished.

Suddenly, as the stage rounded a bend not two miles from High Cactus, Joe Bradley and his guard found themselves confronted by a quartet of masked men blocking their passage. One was clad in a city-style suit, while the others wore long brown-leather coats: all had drawn their revolvers and were aiming them at the approaching stage.

'Halt!' yelled the leader, the man in the city-style suit.

Joe Bradley gritted his teeth and, ignoring the outlaw's command, drove the horses straight at the would-be robbers. As the horses picked up speed, so Mickey Price lifted and aimed his shotgun at the outlaws. But before he could squeeze the trigger, all four fired. One slug smashed into Joe Bradley's shoulder, causing him to cry out and let go of the reins. Half a dozen others struck the hapless young guard in the chest, belly and head, blasting him back against the front of the coach and then toppling him from the box.

As Mickey Price hit the ground, the stagecoach burst through the cordon of outlaws, forcing them to pull their horses to either side of the trail. Recovering, they hastily wheeled round and set off in pursuit.

Scotch John cursed beneath his breath. This was his first attempt at holding up a stagecoach and, following the gang's successful bank robbery in Cripple Creek, he had no wish to experience failure. He forged ahead of his three companions and quickly drew level with the stage. The driver, meantime, had regained the reins and was struggling to control the horses with his left hand, while his right arm hung limply at his side and blood seeped from his shoulder wound. Scotch John did not hesitate, but launched himself at the stage, landing on the box and elbowing Joe Bradley to the side where the guard had previously been sitting. He ripped the reins from Bradley's grasp and began tugging at them. The horses responded and, by the time the Duff brothers and Limpy Harris drew level, he had succeeded in bringing the stagecoach to a halt.

He pulled Bradley's gun from its holster and tossed it into the nearby brush. Then he climbed down off the box and threw open the near-side door of the stagecoach.

'Howdy, folks,' he said. 'You step down nice 'n' easy an' nobody gits hurt. OK?'

'This . . . this is an outrage!' spluttered Horace Potterton, as he reluctantly climbed out of the coach. 'My name is Horace Potterton and I am the mayor of High Cactus. You . . . you shall pay for this!'

'Will I indeed, Mr Potterton? I don't think so.

But you an' your fellow passengers are surely gonna pay. So, hand over your purses an' your wallets.'

'I will not, Mr Whatever-your-name-is.'

'Scotch John MacGregor. An' you will, mister, unless you wanta be pistol-whipped.'

Horace Potterton quailed at this threat, while from his position on the box Joe Bradley mumbled faintly, 'Do as he says, Mr Potterton, for I guess these fellers ain't gonna take no for an answer.'

Scotch John smiled broadly.

'That's good advice,' he said.

'Yes. Please, Horace, don't antagonize them,' pleaded his wife.

'We ain't got no choice but to do as the man says,' added Sidney Squill nervously. 'Look what he an' his gang did to our driver an' his guard.'

Horace Potterton sighed deeply. Pompous and bumptious he might be, yet he was no coward. However, he had no wish to be pistol-whipped in addition to being robbed. He shrugged his shoulders and very unwillingly handed over his wallet. The others followed suit and, immediately thereafter, Scotch John began searching through their luggage. It was as well for him that he did, for he found in Harry Laine's carpetbag a considerable quantity of banknotes. Although his business trip to Pueblo was of an exploratory nature, Laine had deemed it prudent to have some ready cash with him. Now he regretted that decision.

Scotch John emptied the purses and wallets and counted their contents. The haul was not as much as he might have wished, although Harry Laine's contribution had certainly made the hold-up worthwhile.

'OK,' he said. 'Now I want all your valuables: watches, rings, bracelets and so on. In fact, I guess you'd better strip right down to your undergarments,' he added as an afterthought.

This brought forth a host of protests from each and every one of the passengers. Not simply content with robbing them, Scotch John was evidently also intent on humiliating them. He waited until their cries had subsided, before saying quietly, 'That pistol-whippin' I mentioned earlier, it won't be confined to you gents. You all do as I say or the ladies ain't gonna look so pretty.'

'You sonofabitch!' cried Potterton, and he made as though to step forward and launch himself at the outlaw chief.

Before he could do so, however, Nancy grabbed hold of his arm and cried, 'No, Horace! For pity's sake, let's do what he asks!'

'Listen to what Nancy says,' hissed Sidney Squill.

'Yes, do!' added his wife anxiously.

The mayor scowled, but once again allowed himself to be persuaded to accede to Scotch John's demands. Silently and with a very bad grace, the five passengers began to undress. Scotch John turned to order the stagecoach driver to do like-

46

wise, but Joe Bradley had passed out and was sprawled senseless across the box.

Presently, when the five were stripped down to their underclothes, Scotch John collected all their valuables and stuffed them, together with the banknotes he had counted earlier, into his and his accomplices' saddle-bags. Then he gathered up their clothes and distributed them amongst Limpy Harris and the two Duff brothers. They, for their part, hooted with laughter and waved these various articles contemptuously at Horace Potterton and his fellow passengers.

Scotch John mounted his horse and dropped his Colt Peacemaker back into its holster. He smiled and raised his hat towards his victims.

'I'll bid you good day, ladies an' gentlemen,' he cried and, turning his horse's head, galloped off down the winding trail, towards the plain and away from High Cactus.

Limpy Harris and the Duff brothers paused only to whoop and holler triumphantly, before setting off after him. And, indeed, they continued to whoop and holler as they vanished from sight with their ill-gotten gains.

Behind them, the two women collapsed sobbing, while Horace Potterton hurried to the front of the stagecoach, where Joe Bradley lay unconscious on the box. The mayor ripped off his undershirt and, tearing it into strips, set to stanching the blood and then binding the driver's wound. By the time he had finished, Bradley's senses had returned and he was able to sit upright. Sidney Squill and Harry Laine, in the meantime, had brought Mickey Price's body from where it lay sprawled across the trail and laid it down beside the stagecoach. The young shotgun guard's zest for adventure was quenched for ever.

'Can you drive, Joe?' Potterton enquired of the driver.

Bradley, although deathly pale and clearly shaken, slowly nodded his head.

'I guess so, Mr Potterton. We ain't got much more'n a coupla miles to go 'fore we reach town,' he muttered.

'Good man!' said Potterton approvingly. He glanced down at Mickey Price's corpse and then at the others. 'We cain't leave this young feller out here. We must take him into town,' he declared.

'But . . . but I . . . I don't think I could bear to have his b-body inside the coach,' stammered Dorothy Squill.

'Nor I, Horace,' whispered Nancy, her eyes downcast.

'No, of course not, my dear,' said Potterton. 'We'll lift him on to the box and prop him up there 'tween Joe and me.'

'You propose to ride on the box, Horace?' said his wife.

'I do. Sidney and you, sir' – here Potterton addressed the land agent – 'can help me lift his body up there. And, while we're doing that, you ladies might care to climb back inside.'

'Yes, Horace,' said his wife meekly.

She and Dorothy hastened to board the stage-coach, at the same time studiously avoiding looking at Mickey Price's bullet-ridden and bloodied corpse. By the time they were settled inside, the youngster was propped up between Joe Bradley and Horace Potterton and the former had the reins in his left hand, ready to set off. Sidney Squill and the land agent hurriedly clambered aboard and Horace Potterton gave the command.

'Let's go, Joe!' he cried.

The stagecoach rumbled up the incline, travelling at an even slower pace than it had been making immediately prior to the hold-up. Eventually, approximately half a mile outside the town, the trail levelled out and the stage picked up a little speed.

It rattled across the town limits and along Main Street before coming to a halt in front of High Cactus's stage-line depot. Here the appearance of the mayor, the deputy mayor, their ladies and the young land agent, all clad only in their undergarments, at first caused the crowd, which invariably gathered when the stage came into town, to roar with laughter. But the laughter subsided when they observed that the driver had been wounded and his guard shot dead. The town's doctor was quickly summoned to tend to Joe Bradley, while the mortician arrived to take care of the young guard's dead body.

Horace Potterton explained to the sheriff what had befallen them and promised a full statement later. Then he and his wife hurried off towards their home, as did Sidney and Dorothy Squill. However, realizing that Harry Laine was now penniless, the departing mayor directed the land agent to his general store and informed his store assistant, who was standing at the edge of the crowd, that he should clothe Laine free of charge.

Also standing at the edge of the crowd was Simon Laidlaw. He had observed and heard everything and made copious notes. He turned and repaired to his hotel, where he intended converting the notes into a comprehensive report. The *Chicago Daily News* was about to receive his second dispatch.

FOUR

Spring and summer had passed, and it was October and Saturday night in Touchstone, the night the cowhands from the nearby Buena Vista ranch came to town. Some were in the bar-room of the Silver Star Hotel, while the rest had chosen the Last Dime saloon to provide their evening's entertainment.

Also in the Silver Star's bar-room that evening was Scotch John MacGregor. He was disguised as an itinerant cowpoke in a grey Stetson, leather vest, check shirt, Levis and spurred boots. The Stetson was wide-brimmed and pulled fairly low down so as to hide his red hair. The little that did show beneath the brim was cloaked in shadow. He had taken the precaution because his red hair was his main distinguishing feature. While red hair was not unknown in the West, it remained uncommon and Scotch John was taking no chances.

Since he had last been in Touchstone as a boy of

51

fourteen, he reckoned there was little likelihood that anyone in the town who had known him then would recognize him now.

Scotch John's success during the previous months had been due to meticulous planning. Before the gang raided a bank or held up a stagecoach, he reconnoitred the town in which the bank stood, or in which the stagecoach was expected. He had worn this disguise on each occasion since the gang's first bank robbery in Cripple Creek. As he invariably wore his city-style suit when committing his crimes, he felt pretty sure he would pass incognito. The same applied to the rest of the gang. They always wore their long leather coats when holding up stagecoaches, but they, too, donned cowboy attire when entering town to rob a bank. And they varied their manner of entering towns, sometimes riding in together, sometimes in ones and twos. Scotch John maintained that, in this way, they sustained the element of surprise.

Now, on this particular Saturday, he had returned to the town close to which he had spent his childhood holidays. Although Touchstone was the town nearest to his mountain hideout, the outlaw had made a conscious decision to avoid raiding its bank until now, for he had been anxious that nobody should guess in which area of the mountains his retreat lay. The previous raids, dotted here and there across the length and breadth of central Colorado, had served this purpose well and, at the same time, prevented the forces of law and order from guessing where the gang would strike next.

His reconnaissance completed, Scotch John had enjoyed a meal in the hotel restaurant and now was aiming to knock back a couple of beers in the bar-room before returning to his mountain fastness.

He sidled up to the bar, where two of the cowhands from the Buena Vista ranch were standing, drinking beer and smoking cheroots. They were among several of Touchstone's townsfolk crowded round the bar. Most of their fellow cowhands were in the Last Dime saloon, while the few others present were either playing blackjack or were upstairs with the Silver Star's sporting women.

Randy Oates, a tall, lanky, weatherbeaten forty-year-old and Larry Parr, a short, squat fellow with a neat white beard and whiskers, pushing sixty, were respectively the ranch's top hand and its cook. They were deep in conversation. Scotch John had never seen the cook before, but his uncle had pointed out the top hand on several occasions as he and his nephews passed the ranch on one of their many hunting expeditions. There was little chance, however, that Randy Oates would recognize him, for he had changed considerably in the passing years and, anyway, they had never actually been introduced to each other.

'Is Lloyd likely to join us tonight?' shouted a large, red-faced man from his seat at the bar-room's sole poker table, breaking into the two ranch hands' conversation.

'No, Bill, he ain't,' replied Randy Oates shortly.

'That's a coupla weeks now he's missed,' commented the red-faced man.

'Yeah. Mebbe he'll make it next week,' said Oates.

'I hope so.'

The red-faced man returned his attention to the game, while Oates muttered, 'It's a shame, the boss bein' confined the way he is to the ranch. He sure used to enjoy his Saturday night game of poker.'

'Yeah. An' all because of the activities of that there Scotch John MacGregor an' his gang,' remarked Larry Parr. 'The sooner those varmints are caught the better.'

'Darned right.'

Scotch John was intrigued. Why in tarnation, he wondered, should his exploits cause the owner of the Buena Vista ranch to remain there on a Saturday night, rather than ride into town to participate in what was evidently a regular poker game? Well, there was only one way to find out. He would have to ask.

'Pardon me,' he said, 'but I couldn't help over-hearin' what you was sayin'.'

'Yeah?'

'Yeah I've jest rode in from Castle Rock, where

54

Scotch John held up the bank a few days back. An' I'm kinda curious to know why your boss would pass up a reg'lar poker game on account of him. I mean, Scotch John ain't likely to raid his ranch, surely? He's a bank robber, not a cattle rustler.'

Randy Oates grinned.

'Mr Whittle don't see it that way,' he said.

'No?'

'No. Y'see, Mrs Whittle, she's recently given birth to a daughter.'

'So? I cain't see that Scotch John is likely to be much of a threat to either mother or daughter.'

'Tell him,' said Larry Parr.

'Yeah, let me explain, stranger,' said Oates. 'It's like this. Mrs Whittle's younger sister Fiona, she came out West to help Mrs Whittle both durin' an' after the birth. Now Fiona's father is James Randall, the railroad magnate, an' he was dead set against her leavin' Chicago an' headin' out here. The news of Scotch John's exploits is, it seems, in all the newspapers an' he figured it was too dangerous for his younger daughter to travel out to Colorado. But she's an independent, head-strong young lady, an' she jest went ahead an' defied him an' came anyway.'

'Ah!' said Scotch John. 'I begin to see.'

'Mr Whittle told me that James Randall was furious an' has forbidden Fiona to leave the ranch, although she's no longer needed by Mrs Whittle.

55

He's scared that, if'n she does, Scotch John an' his gang might hold up either the stagecoach or train she's travellin' in an' kidnap her.'

'So, she is confined to the ranch until Scotch John is apprehended?'

'Either until then or until James Randall can spare the time to come an' fetch her. I figure he's makin' her cool her heels, to teach her a lesson. But, in due course, he's expected to turn up here with an armed escort.'

'He's not afraid, then, that she'll defy him a second time an' return to Chicago unescorted?'

Randy Oates laughed.

'No,' he said. 'He has told the boss to make sure she doesn't leave Buena Vista till he arrives. Which is why the boss doesn't leave the ranch on Saturday nights. He feels responsible for the li'l lady an' he's the kinda man that takes his responsibilities seriously.'

'Yeah. Didn't he give Mr Randall his word that he'd watch over her night an' day?' enquired Parr.

'He did, Larry, an' he's a man of his word,' averred the top hand.

'Wa'al, seems to me both your boss an' Mr Randall are bein' a mite over-protective,' commented Scotch John.

'I feel the same,' said Oates, 'but, then, I ain't a father nor even an uncle.'

'Me neither,' said Scotch John.

'Like I said, it's a shame,' declared Oates. 'The

boss always enjoyed his weekly game of poker. A man has to relax a li'l sometimes,' he added philosophically.

'Wa'al, let's hope that Mr Randall turns up pretty soon,' said Scotch John.

'Or that Scotch John is taken by the law,' said Parr.

'Even better,' agreed Oates.

' 'Course,' said Scotch John, smiling inwardly and crossing his fingers behind his back.

'So, you lookin' for ranch work, stranger?' enquired Oates, by way of changing the subject.

'No, I got me a job lined up on a ranch some ways north of here, in Montana,' lied the outlaw.

'Good cattle country,' commented Oates.

'Yeah.'

'So you're jest passin' through,' said Parr.

'That's right. I figure I'll have one more beer 'fore I ride out. You gents care to join me?' asked Scotch John.

'That's mighty civil of you,' said Oates.

'Sure is. Thanks,' added Parr.

Scotch John finished the beer he had been drinking and ordered three more. Then, when the beers arrived, the three men toasted each other and proceeded to quaff them.

A quarter of an hour later, Scotch John left the hotel, unhitched his coal-black mare from the rail outside and headed off down Main Street in the direction of the Sangre de Cristo mountains.

Earlier, he had carefully reconnoitred the town of Touchstone with a view to robbing its bank, but now he had a different plan in mind.

FIVE

It was early on the Saturday evening following Scotch John MacGregor's brief visit to the town and Touchstone's sheriff was sitting in his office reading the latest edition of the *Denver News*.

Joe Norris had been sheriff for more years than he cared to remember. Retirement beckoned, something to which he was looking forward. One more year and he could hand over the task of maintaining law and order to somebody else. Grey-haired and world-weary, he had perforce to wear spectacles to read the newspaper.

The piece which Norris was perusing caused the law officer to scowl. It had been written by Simon Laidlaw and was published by the *Denver News*, one of the syndicate of newspapers reporting on the exploits of Scotch John MacGregor and his gang. This latest story concerned the gang's raid, a flew days earlier, upon the Cattlemen's Bank in Castle Rock, a small cattle town not twenty miles away.

59

The gang, it seemed, had escaped unscathed, but both the bank manager and his teller had attempted to resist and, in consequence, had been shot and killed.

Sheriff Joe Norris reflected grimly that, in the last six months, Scotch John and his gang had carried out no fewer than four bank robberies and held up a total of six stagecoaches, all within the state of Colorado. And a dozen people had been killed and sixteen wounded during the course of these stick-ups.

Norris assumed that, sooner or later, the outlaws would inevitably target Touchstone, unless they were taken by the forces of law and order before they could do so. Certainly, the state was teeming with US marshals, county sheriffs, town marshals, their deputies and several bounty hunters, all searching desperately for Scotch John and his gang. But to search Colorado's vast wilderness, with its huge expanses of forest and mountain, was an almost hopeless task. To discover the outlaws' hideaway, the lawmen would require an extremely large slice of luck. And Joe Norris was doubtful whether they would get it.

As these pessimistic thoughts drifted through the sheriff's mind, the door of the law office was suddenly thrown open and Deputy Tim Bannon burst in. Tall and gangly, with a youthful countenance and engaging manner, Bannon was both young and enthusiastic.

'Sheriff! he cried. 'We got trouble in the Last Dime!'

'Them cowpokes from the Buena Vista?' growled Norris.

'Yup.'

'Hmm. I wish to hell Mr Whittle'd git rid of that sister-in-law of his so's he could ride into town on Saturday nights. His boys ain't nowhere near so much trouble when their boss is in town,' remarked Joe Norris glumly.

'No, they ain't,' agreed Tim Bannon.

'Wa'al, I s'pose we'd best git over there an' quieten things down,' muttered the sheriff.

He laid down his spectacles, picked up his hat and followed the deputy out of the law office. The sounds of the affray emanating from the Last Dime were loud and raucous. Joe Norris swore beneath his breath and headed slowly towards the saloon.

While Touchstone's sheriff and his deputy were engaged in quelling the fracas at the Last Dime saloon, Scotch John MacGregor and the Duff brothers were waiting in the foothills, a mere two miles outside the boundary of the Buena Vista ranch. For a week the gang had been keeping a surreptitious watch on the ranch and all its comings and goings. They waited anxiously, Scotch John astride his black mare and holding the reins of a spare horse, ready saddled.

Presently, they heard the sound of a horse's

61

hoofs and Limpy Harris rode up out of the darkness.

'Wa'al?' snapped Scotch John.

'The cowpokes left the ranch as they usually do on a Saturday night,' reported Harris.

'All of 'em?'

'All except their boss. I followed 'em into town. They're all either drinkin', gamblin' or whorin'. They won't be leavin' Touchstone any time soon.'

'Good!' Scotch John smiled broadly. He was ready to put his new plan into operation. Its feasibility had depended upon Fiona Randall remaining at the Buena Vista. All week he had been anxious lest her father should turn up to escort her back to Chicago. Which was why he had kept the ranch under constant surveillance since his visit to Touchstone the previous Saturday. 'OK, let's go,' he said.

'One minute, boss,' said Limpy Harris. 'A thought jest struck me.'

'Oh, yeah?' Scotch John didn't sound too interested.

'Yeah. Your plan is to kidnap Mr Whittle's sister-in-law, the gal who recently came out here from Chicago, right?'

'Yup. Her father, James Randall, is stinkin' rich. He'll be sure to pay a large ransom for her safe return.'

'Then, why don't we also kidnap her sister, the rancher's wife? We could then demand twice the ransom. After all, they're both Mr Randall's daughters.'

Scotch John shook his head.

'No, I don't think so. Mrs Whittle has not long since given birth, an' I ain't about to separate mother an' baby.' While his associates were concerned only with the loot, he was equally concerned with his reputation. He craved fame as an audacious, devil-may-care outlaw and he felt that abducting the young mother would inevitably tarnish his image. Besides, the ransom he proposed to ask for Fiona Randall's safe return was pretty enormous, and this, added to their previous ill-gotten gains, would make all four of them rich men. 'Let's not be too greedy,' he said.

'But, boss—'

'I'm gonna ask for two hundred thousand dollars.'

'For Miss Randall?'

'Yup. Ain't that enough for you, Limpy?'

'It is for me!' gasped Dan Duff.

'An' for me,' exclaimed his brother.

'Wa'al, Limpy?'

Limpy Harris had certainly not anticipated such a large figure.

'Yeah, I guess so,' he conceded.

'Right. Then, unless anyone else has got somethin' to say, let's go!' cried Scotch John.

The four outlaws rode down from the foothills, Scotch John leading the spare horse. They cantered across the plain towards the Buena Vista. As they reached the gateway to the ranch, they could see lights showing in the ranch house. Scotch John guessed that the rancher, his wife and her sister were probably having supper. He lifted his hand to bring the cavalcade to a halt.

'OK,' he murmured. 'We dismount an' approach the ranch house on foot. Limpy, you remain here with the horses. I'll call when I need you to bring 'em up to the house.'

'Sure, boss.'

'I wanta take 'em by surprise. I want no shootin' an' no killin'. We need to take Miss Randall alive. You got that, boys?'

'We got it,' said Dan Duff, while Nick Duff merely nodded.

'Then, we dismount. Now.'

Scotch John swung himself out of the saddle and the two brothers straightaway followed suit. Only Limpy Harris remained mounted.

The three men cautiously tiptoed through the gateway towards the distant ranch house. Nobody spoke until they were within a few yards of the building. Then they drew their guns from their holsters and Scotch John whispered, 'Wait here. I'll wave when I want you.'

'Do we pull up our masks?' enquired Dan Duff.

'I don't think we need to bother,' replied Scotch John, 'for I figure this'll be our last job. Then it'll be goodbye, Colorado.'

He ran soundlessly across the short distance to the stoop; then, crouching low, he proceeded to climb the flight of wooden steps leading up to it. Stealthily, he crept towards the nearest lighted window. He raised his head a few inches and took a quick peek. Then he lowered his head again. He had seen enough. Lloyd Whittle, his wife Jessica and her sister Fiona were all sitting round the rancher's dining-table, enjoying their supper. None of them had spotted him.

Scotch John waved to his two accomplices. Moments later, all three stood before the ranch house door.

'In we go!' rasped Scotch John.

He was the first through the doorway, slamming the door wide open and aiming his Colt Peacemaker at Lloyd Whittle, who was sitting at the head of the table, his sister-in-law on his left. Jessica Whittle, meantime, had gone into her bedroom to check that her baby daughter was asleep. Fiona Randall's frightened scream brought her rushing back into the room.

'What the blue blazes—?' began Lloyd Whittle, as he leapt to his feet.

'Shuddup!' snapped Scotch John.

The rancher, a tall, broad-shouldered man in his late thirties, flushed angrily. His eyes glinted and his jaw tightened. Had he been carrying a gun, he would undoubtedly have attempted to draw it, in which case Scotch John would have had no option

65

other than to shoot him. It was fortunate, therefore, that Lloyd Whittle was unarmed.

The two young sisters, Jessica twenty-three and Fiona, two years her junior, stared in horror at the intruders. Both were brunettes, with slender figures and pretty faces. However, those faces were drained of colour and their beautiful blue eyes wide with fear.

Fiona Randall's scream had disturbed the baby, whose cries now emanated from the bedroom.

'I must tend to my child,' Jessica informed the outlaws and, before Scotch John could protest, she vanished into the bedroom. He made as though to follow her, but had taken only a couple of steps when Jessica reappeared, with her baby daughter cradled in her arms.

'OK,' said Lloyd Whittle, 'tell us what you want?'

He spoke quietly, anxiously, for he had guessed the purpose of the raid. He figured that his father-in-law's worst fears had just been realized.

'We want her,' said Scotch John, staring hard at Fiona.

Then, while the Duff brothers levelled their guns at the rancher, he dropped his own gun back into its holster and grabbed hold of the girl.

'No!' she screamed and promptly set Jessica's child crying again.

'Shuddup all of you!' roared Scotch John, and he slapped the girl hard across the cheek, effectively silencing her.

In the meantime, Jessica had once more succeeded in quietening her young daughter. She gently rocked the baby, while Fiona collapsed limply in the outlaw's iron grasp and sobbed tearfully, yet soundlessly.

'What . . . what d'you intend doin' with Fiona?' demanded Whittle. 'Why d'you want her?'

Scotch John grinned sardonically.

'I reckon you know why we want her, Mr Whittle,' he said.

'You intend holding her to ransom?'

'Yup.'

'Oh, no! Please, no!' cried Fiona.

'We ain't gonna hurt you, providin' you don't give us no trouble,' said Scotch John. Then he added in a menacing tone, 'An' providin' your daddy pays us the ransom we demand.'

'How much?' growled Whittle.

'Two hundred thousand dollars.'

The rancher's jaw dropped, while the two young women both gasped. The outlaw's demand was much greater than any of them could have anticipated.

'That's crazy!' stated Whittle.

'Yes. Pa won't pay that much! He just won't!' exclaimed Fiona.

'Oh, I reckon he will!' said Scotch John. 'He ain't got no choice if'n he wants you returned to him safe an' sound. What do you say, Mr Whittle?'

Lloyd Whittle scowled.

'I guess your pa *will* pay, Fiona,' he muttered glumly.

'But I came out here against his will,' cried Fiona.

'Even so. He won't abandon you, sister dear,' said Jessica.

'Oh, Jessica!'

'Bear up. Pa will pay this villain what he demands and you'll be set free.' Tears streaming down her cheeks, Jessica turned to face Scotch John. 'You promise you won't harm her?' she entreated him.

'You have the word of Scotch John MacGregor,' said the outlaw solemnly. 'Like I said, if'n the li'l lady behaves herself an' her daddy stumps up them two hundred thousand dollars, she ain't got nuthin' to fear. 'Course, should any attempt be made to follow us into the mountains, I'd surely kill her. An' believe me, that's no idle threat. All activities designed to hunt down an' apprehend me an' my gang must cease forthwith.'

'You sonofabitch!' snarled Whittle.

Jessica grabbed his arm and murmured, 'Careful, Lloyd. Don't antagonize him.'

'Yeah, jest watch your tongue,' Scotch John warned him.

The rancher glared at the red-haired outlaw, but contented himself with growling, 'So, what happens next?'

'That's easy,' said Scotch John. 'Me an' the boys

ride off with Miss Randall an' you head into Touchstone, where you wire Mr James Randall. You'll inform him that Scotch John MacGregor has his daughter Fiona an' that he can have her back safe an' sound for the sum of two hundred thousand dollars. He's to bring that sum to Touchstone an' await my instructions.'

'An' jest how are you aimin' to give my father-in-law those instructions?'

'I'll allow him three days to gather together the money an' make the journey to Touchstone. Then I'll send one of my boys into town. He'll issue Mr Randall with the necessary orders. You can tell Mr Randall to book into the Silver Star Hotel. My man will contact him there. That clear?'

'Perfectly.'

'In that case, I'll bid you good evenin'.'

Scotch John turned and dragged a loudly protesting Fiona Randall across the room and out through the open doorway. The Duff brothers quickly followed, though they backed out, their guns all the while trained on Lloyd Whittle and his wife, neither of whom moved until the two desperadoes had disappeared outside.

By the time Lloyd Whittle ventured out on to the stoop, Scotch John and the others were already on their way to where Limpy Harris awaited them. Scotch John heaved the girl up on to the back of the spare horse. Then, once he was certain she was secure in the saddle, he mounted his mare and, taking hold of the spare horse's bridle, led Fiona Randall off in the wake of his three associates. Meantime, Whittle stood helpless upon the stoop and watched them vanish into the darkness, *en route* to the distant mountains.

'Oh, Lloyd!' gasped his wife. 'What are we to do?'

'What that feller callin' hisself Scotch John told us to do,' replied Whittle tersely.

'Hmm. Yeah, I guess so.' Jessica rocked her daughter, who had again drifted off to sleep. 'But . . . but can we trust Scotch John to keep his end of the bargain?' she asked anxiously.

'I dunno, though we gotta hope so for Fiona's sake.'

'Yes.'

'I'll saddle up an' ride into town.'

'You . . . you ain't gonna leave me here alone with our baby daughter?'

'Them outlaws ain't likely to return.'

I . . . I know. But they scared me witless. And I couldn't bear to be left here on my own.'

'OK. I'll hitch up the buckboard an' we'll ride into town on that.'

'Gee, thanks, Lloyd!'

A much relieved Jessica Whittle continued to rock her sleeping child, while the rancher hastily hitched a couple of horses to the buckboard and brought it round to the front of the ranch house. Moments later, they were on their way to town.

70

As the buckboard rolled into Touchstone, Sheriff Joe Norris and Deputy Tim Bannon emerged from the Last Dime saloon. They had a firm hold of two drunken cowboys. They had succeeded in breaking up the fracas inside the saloon and restoring order. Now they were in the process of marching the two main offenders across the street to the law office, where the cowboys were destined to spend the night in one of its cells.

However, the sight of Lloyd Whittle and his wife and daughter galloping into town and pulling up in front of their office caused the lawmen to let go of their prisoners, who promptly staggered a few steps and collapsed in a drunken heap.

'Mr Whittle, what in tarnation are you an' Mrs Whittle doin', ridin' into town in such a rush?' enquired Norris.

' We've been raided by Scotch John MacGregor an' his gang!' replied the rancher.

'Yes. And they've taken Fiona!' cried Jessica.

'Taken your sister! Where?'

'To their lair up in the mountains, the hideaway every lawman in Colorado has been searchin' for these last six months,' said Whittle angrily.

'Holy cow!'

'Scotch John is demanding that my father pay him two hundred thousand dollars for Fiona's safe return,' explained Jessica.

Both the sheriff and his deputy looked at each other and whistled.

'Can . . . can your father raise that kinda money?' asked Norris.

'I guess so,' said Jessica.

'Wowee!' yelled one of the small crowd, who had followed the sheriff out of the saloon and was now gathered in the street outside the law office.

'Somebody's gotta catch them murderin', no-account sonsofbitches!' shouted another townsman.

'Yeah. What are we payin' our taxes for,' demanded the proprietor of Touchstone's general store, 'if'n Scotch John an' his bunch of miscreants can come an' go as they darned well please?'

'Seems all the sheriff's good for is arrestin' a few drunken cowpokes,' commented the town's barber.

'Hell, that ain't fair!' rasped Sheriff Joe Norris.

'No, it ain't!' agreed his deputy warmly.

'Yes, it is!'

As the argument raged, Simon Laidlaw, who had been on the fringe of the crowd, quietly slipped away. He had heard enough.

The latest telegram from his cousin had reached him in Colorado Springs three days earlier. It had read as follows: *Be at the Silver Star Hotel in Touchstone by Saturday next. Could be the last time. Rob Roy.*

Naturally, Laidlaw had expected that he would be reporting either a bank robbery in Touchstone or a stagecoach hold-up outside the town. He had certainly not expected to be reporting a kidnapping. He smiled to himself. The size of the ransom explained why Scotch John had included the phrase, *Could be the last time* in his wire.

The young reporter repaired to his hotel room, where he set about composing what was likely to be his penultimate dispatch; in all, his eleventh wire to the *Chicago Daily News.*

SIX

Two days after Fiona Randall's abduction, Pinkerton agent Dave Lansom descended from the mid-afternoon train and walked into the town where Scotch John had conducted his last bank raid. Castle Rock was, like Touchstone, a small cattle town, and stood some twenty miles away to the north. Lansom aimed to take a room at the town's Pine Tree Hotel, but first he wanted to speak to the sheriff. Consequently, he headed for the law office.

It was over two weeks since the bank robbery and Dave Lansom was only too well aware that the trail would probably be cold by now. Nevertheless, it was a starting point.

The delay in dispatching the Pinkerton agent was due entirely to procrastination on the part of the board of the Cattlemen's Bank. Of the four banks robbed by Scotch John and his gang, three had been Cattlemen's Banks. Up until the latest raid, the board had been content to leave the pursuit of the outlaws to the official law enforcement agencies: the US marshals, the county sheriffs and the town marshals. The raid at Castle Rock had changed that policy. But it had taken some little time before enough members of the board were convinced that they should employ their own private investigator. It was at this point that they consulted the Pinkerton Detective Agency.

Dave Lansom was a slim, elegant thirty-year-old. His youthful looks, innocent blue eyes and easy manner belied the detective's toughness and natural astuteness. His success rate as an investigator was second to none within the Agency. Indeed, the founder, Allan Pinkerton, had hand-picked him for this particular assignment. Attired in a low-crowned black Stetson, black frock-coat, vest and matching trousers, neat white shirt and bootlace tie, and wearing a pair of highly polished black shoes, he looked every inch the city gent. He had, however, packed both boots and spurs in case he should have occasion to proceed on horseback, and he carried a long-barrelled .30-calibre Colt revolver in a shoulder rig beneath his coat.

Lansom pushed open the law office door and stepped inside. He dumped his luggage on the floor and raised his hat.

'Howdy, Sheriff,' he said, addressing the peace officer, who was sitting behind a large desk and casually studying a sheaf of Wanted notices.

Sheriff Sam Shaw looked up and smiled. Several years younger than his fellow lawman in Touchstone, he was a big, heavily built man in his mid-forties, full of vigour and still in his prime. He half-rose, stretched out a hand and warmly shook that of the Pinkerton agent.

'Howdy, Mr Lansom,' he said.

Dave Lansom gazed at the sheriff in surprise.

'You know my name! You were expectin' me?' he asked.

'Yup. Your boss wired me. He said that the Pinkerton Detective Agency had been engaged by the Cattlemen's Bank to hunt down Scotch John MacGregor an' his gang. An', since this is where their last raid took place, it was to Castle Rock that you were headin'.'

'That's right. But Mr Pinkerton needn't have wired you, for I was aimin' to call in an' introduce myself.'

'Yeah, wa'al, he has a message, which he wanted me to give you.'

'A message?'

'Yup. He said to tell you that you're to hold fire on your investigation an' do nuthin' till you receive further instructions from him. He's gonna wire me an' let me know when you can go ahead.'

'I don't understand. The longer I delay, the less chance I have of trackin' down those murderin' varmints.'

Sheriff Sam Shaw smiled sympathetically.

'I agree,' he said. 'But things have changed since you set out. A few hours after you left Chicago, the MacGregor gang abducted a young woman from a ranch jest outside Touchstone.'

'So?'

'The young woman in question is Fiona Randall, younger daughter of the railway magnate, James Randall She was there, visitin' her sister who had had a baby. The gang have demanded that a ransom of two hundred thousand dollars be brought to Touchstone, an' they've threatened should anyone come lookin' for the girl, they'll kill her.'

'Bluff.'

'Mebbe, but Mr Randall ain't takin' no chances.'

'Whaddya mean?'

'He wants a halt put on all attempts to hunt down Scotch John an' his gang until such time as his daughter is released.'

'He's gonna pay the ransom?'

'He is.'

'Goddammit, he's crazy! You cain't do business with those scum.'

Again Sam Shaw smiled sympathetically.

'I'm inclined to agree, but, then, it ain't my daughter who's been abducted.'

'No,' said Lansom. 'I guess mebbe I'd feel the same if I were in his shoes. So, what about the US marshals an' other folks out lookin' for the outlaws? Have they stopped searchin'?'

'As far as I can understand, yes. Y'see, Mr Randall is a mighty rich an' influential feller. 'Deed, it's said he's a close personal friend of the President, no less.'

'The President of the United States?' exclaimed Lansom.

'The same. An' Mr Lansom has got the President to decree that no further action be taken against the outlaw until after his daughter is freed. I tell you, Mr Lansom, the telegraph wires across the length an' breadth of this here state have sure been buzzin' these last few days.'

'An' d'you reckon all those out lookin' for Scotch John have been recalled?' enquired the Pinkerton man.

Sam Shaw shook his head.

'Not quite,' he said. 'I had instructions to keep a look-out for you an' one other feller.'

'Oh, yeah?'

'Does the name Jack Stone mean anythin' to you?'

Dave Lansom nodded. He had, over the years, conducted several investigations out West and, during the course of them, had often heard the name mentioned.

'The man who tamed Mallory,' said Lansom.

'Ah, so you have heard of him!' remarked the sheriff. 'A livin' legend, he's been many things in his time: Army scout, deputy US marshal, deputy sheriff, guard on the Overland stage, buckaroo on several cattle drives. Hell, there ain't much Jack Stone ain't done!'

'Seems not.'

'It was tamin' Mallory, the roughest, toughest town in the whole of this here state of Colorado, that made his name. State Governor Bill Watson brought Stone in to do that job. I'm told the Governor an' Stone were old comrades-in-arms.'

'Where's this leadin'?' enquired Lansom.

'Governor Watson has hired him a second time.'

'To hunt down the MacGregor gang?'

'Yup. Stone's been out searchin' for 'em for some li'l time. But where exactly he is, nobody knows. The Governor wants him to hold fire for the time bein', jest like the rest of us. An' I guess he's wired every law office in the state with instructions to look out for him an' pass on that message.'

'Will he obey, assumin' he does in fact receive the message?'

'I dunno.' Shaw scratched his head. 'He won't wanta, that's for sure.'

'Wa'al, neither do I.'

'No.'

'How long d'you reckon it'll be 'fore James Randall turns up in Touchstone with the ransom money?'

'Today? Tomorrow? Pretty darned soon. Seems Scotch John is aimin' to send one of his men into town tomorrow. He gave Mr Randall till then to arrive with the money. I figure Mr Randall will try to keep to that deadline.'

'An unfortunate choice of word, Sheriff.'

Shaw frowned.

'Yeah, guess it was,' he admitted dolefully. 'Anyways, it's expected that James Randall will arrive in Touchstone tomorrow at the latest.'

'So, if I'm to hunt down those outlaws before he hands over all that money, I'd best git goin',' stated Lansom.

'You ain't goin' nowhere, mister,' retorted the lawman.

'Look, jest pretend you ain't seen me.'

'I cain't do that.'

'You can.'

'All right, I can. But I won't.'

'You're gonna simply sit here an' let that bastard pick up his ransom? An', at the same time, you're gonna prevent me doin' somethin' to stop him?'

'Them's the President's an' the Governor's orders, an' I ain't about to flout 'em. If'n I do an', as a result, Miss Fiona Randall gits killed—'

'Scotch John will likely grab the money an' kill her anyway!'

'Mebbe so. The fact remains: you ain't leavin' town till everythin' is all done an' dusted. The Pine Tree Hotel ain't too bad a place to stay; so, if I was you, I'd mosey on over there an' make your stay in Castle Rock as pleasant as possible.'

Dave Lansom quietly reviewed the situation and

came to the conclusion that he had little or no choice. Should he attempt to flee Castle Rock, he would undoubtedly be prevented from doing so by the sheriff or one of his deputies. In any event, he reflected, the matter of the ransom would likely be settled within the next forty-eight hours.

'OK,' he said resignedly. 'I'll book into that there hotel. Will you let me know when the ransom has been paid an' I'm free to leave Castle Rock?'

'Of course.'

The two men shook hands. Dave Lansom picked up his luggage and, while the sheriff held the door open, promptly left the law office. The door closed behind him and Sam Shaw returned to his perusal of the various Wanted notices.

The Pinkerton agent paused on the stoop outside and looked about him. There were plenty of people hustling and bustling up and down Main Street: cowboys, homesteaders and a variety of traders, some on horseback, some on wagons and some in gigs and buckboards.

Lansom was poised to cross the busy thoroughfare to the hotel opposite when he observed the big man hitching his bay gelding to the rail outside the law office.

The newcomer looked older than his thirty-odd years, for his rugged, square-cut face was deeply lined and his thick brown hair was liberally flecked with grey. Six-foot two-inches in his stockinged feet

81

and consisting of nigh on 200 pounds of muscle and bone, he bore the scars, both mental and physical, of his turbulent and often unhappy life. The bullet holes had healed, but the broken nose remained and the emotional scars, which had made Jack Stone what he was, would never completely heal.

He wore a red kerchief round his thick, strong neck, a grey Stetson, a knee-length buckskin jacket over his grey shirt, faded denim pants over unspurred boots and, tied down on his right thigh, a Frontier Model Colt. Stone looked, and was, a hard man to cross.

As he watched the big man mount the steps to the stoop, the Pinkerton agent had a sudden prescience.

'Pardon me,' he addressed the stranger, 'but would you, by any chance, be Mr Jack Stone?'

The big man regarded Lansom with his cool blue eyes.

'What's it to you?' he growled

'The name's Dave Lansom an' I'm a Pinkerton man. I believe we're both engaged upon the same business.'

'An' what business might that be?'

'The business of apprehendin' Scotch John MacGregor an' his gang.'

The famous Kentuckian gunfighter smiled wryly.

'Yeah, I'm Stone, but I ain't had so much as a sniff

of them outlaws,' he confessed. 'How about you?'

'I've only jest arrived out West.' Lansom glanced towards the law office. 'You figurin' on payin' the sheriff a visit?' he asked.

'Sure. Don't reckon he'll be of much help, but, since Castle Rock's where those no-account critters made their last raid, I s'pose it won't do no harm to have a word with him.'

'Oh, yes, it might!' retorted Lansom.

'Whaddya mean?' demanded Stone.

'Delay your visit to the sheriff an' I'll explain,' said Lansom. 'I'm about to check into the Pine Tree Hotel across the street. Follow me over there an' meet me in the bar-room.'

Jack Stone stared hard at the Pinkerton man. Eventually he muttered, 'You got some kinda badge?'

Dave Lansom produced a neat printed card bearing his name and confirming that he was an agent of the Pinkerton Detective Agency. He handed the card to the Kentuckian. Stone studied it carefully, then handed it back.

'OK,' he said. 'I'll meet you in the bar-room.'

While Dave Lansom headed across Main Street, avoiding the traffic which milled up and down the thoroughfare, Jack Stone unhitched the bay gelding. He quickly climbed into the saddle and, turning the horse's head, trotted off in the wake of the Pinkerton man.

By the time Stone had hitched the gelding to

the rail outside the hotel and made his way inside, Dave Lansom had booked in and was upstairs disposing of his luggage. Consequently, it was the Kentuckian who was first into the bar-room. He ordered a beer and took it across the room to a small, unoccupied corner table.

A few minutes later, Dave Lansom entered. He spotted the Kentuckian and, having also ordered a beer, carried it across the bar-room to the corner table, where he promptly sat down.

'OK,' said Stone. 'What did you mean when you said that me callin' on the sheriff could do some harm?'

'You remarked that the outlaws' raid here in Castle Rock was their latest. Right?'

'That's what I heard.'

'So did I, before I left Chicago. But it ain't.'

'No?'

'No. Since robbin' the bank in Castle Rock, Scotch John an' his gang have struck again.'

'Where?'

'At a ranch jest outside Touchstone.'

'That ain't so far from here. 'Bout twenty miles, I guess. But why in tarnation would they raid a ranch? Have they taken to cattle-rustlin'?'

'No, Mr Stone, they ain't. They've taken to kidnappin'.'

'Holy cow!'

'Seems they abducted Miss Fiona Randall, the younger daughter of the railway magnate, James

Randall, She was visitin' her sister who'd recently had a baby.'

'Wa'al, what are we waitin' for? Let's ride over to Touchstone straightaway.'

'I cain't.'

'Why not?'

'The sheriff won't let me leave town.' Lansom smiled grimly, and went on to explain to Stone about James Randall's fears and the decree, from both the President of the United States and the Governor of Colorado, that all lawmen who were in pursuit of the MacGregor gang should cease their activities forthwith. 'Until the ransom is paid an' Miss Randall is delivered to her father safe an' sound,' he concluded.

'This is crazy!' growled Stone.

'Exactly what I said,' agreed Lansom. 'But that's the way it is. You report to the sheriff an' he will order you to remain in town, too.'

'Which is why you didn't want me to call upon him?'

'Correct. He don't know you're here in Castle Rock, so you can leave any time you like.'

'You reckon I should continue to search for Scotch John an' his gang in defiance of the President's an' the Governor's orders?'

'I do. S'pose James Randall does hand over the ransom which Scotch John has demanded, that don't mean the outlaw will keep his end of the bargain.'

85

'No, I guess not.' Stone rubbed his jaw and carefully considered the situation. 'Reckon I'd best keep lookin' for 'em,' he said at last.

'You ain't had much luck so far, have you?' commented Lansom.

'Nope. Cain't say I have. Learned my trackin' skills off a Kiowa brave, but, so far, I ain't found no trace of 'em. I'm pretty sure they're holed up some place in the Sangre de Cristo mountains, but that's one helluva territory to cover. The entire US Army could look for a year an' still not find 'em.'

'So, you figure your chances of rescuin' Miss Randall 'fore her daddy pays up are kinda slim.'

'Yeah, though I gotta try.'

'Then, how about we work together?'

'But you're confined here in Castle Rock, Mr Lansom.'

'The name's Dave, Mr Stone.'

'An' mine's Jack. OK, so now we're on first name terms, yet where does that git us?'

'Nowhere. It's jest a mite more friendly.'

'Wa'al, then, Dave. . . .'

'There's one angle which I believe nobody's yet considered,' said the Pinkerton agent.

'Go on.'

'Up till now all that's happened is more an' more lawmen have taken off into the mountains without a clue as to the whereabouts of the outlaws' hideout. This because there's no discernible pattern to their raids. Scotch John an' his associates have criss-crossed the state, holdin' up a stage here an' robbin' a bank there, in no partickler order.'

'So?'

'We approach this matter from that other angle I mentioned.'

'An' what is this angle?' growled Stone.

'Let me begin at the beginning,' said Lansom. 'When my boss, Allan Pinkerton, handed me the case, he showed me the various editions of the *Chicago Daily News* in which Scotch John MacGregor's exploits had been reported. He told me that identical reports had appeared in newspapers throughout the United States, from New York to Boston, from Frisco to Los Angeles. And all of these reports had been published within 'bout twenty-four hours of each robbery.'

'How in blue blazes. . . ?'

'There has to be jest the one reporter. He wires his story to one of the newspapers an' that paper syndicates it among all the others.'

'Yeah, I guess that makes sense. But how d'you find out which is the original paper?'

'By askin'. I made me an appointment with the editor of the *Chicago Daily News* an' I struck lucky. It was his reporter. He was none too keen to tell me anythin'. But I persuaded him. I pointed out that, durin' the course of their various robberies, Scotch John an' his gang had murdered no fewer than a dozen innocent folks, an' I asked him if'n he wanted the deaths of any more people on his conscience. He didn't like that an' claimed his conscience was clear. But I then pointed out that, for those reports to have been published so soon after each robbery, his reporter had to have had advance notice of when an' where each robbery was gonna take place.'

'Yeah. That's a good point.'

'The editor thought so, too. Especially when I said he oughta have got in touch with either the US marshals' office, or some other law enforcement agency, down here in Colorado, an' put them on to his reporter. I added that, unless he put *me* on to his reporter, I'd be havin' a word with someone at the US marshals' office.'

'I bet he didn't like that.'

'No, he did not, but he knew he had no choice. So, very reluctantly, he gave me both the name an' a description of his source. The feller is one of his junior reporters, name of Simon Laidlaw.' Lansom paused, took a swig of his beer and continued, 'I asked him where Mr Laidlaw was based, but he reckoned he didn't know. Since each report was telegraphed from the town where the crime was committed, he could be tellin' the truth.'

'Did he know how Laidlaw always managed to be on the spot each time?'

'When I pushed him, he admitted he had a theory about that. It seems that six months back Laidlaw got a cryptic telegram, requestin' that he travel at once to Cripple Creek, Colorado, an' statin' that a big story was about to break down there. He showed the telegram to his editor an' the editor agreed he should go. The bank robbery at Cripple Creek was the MacGregor gang's first. An' that wire was sent by somebody callin' hisself "Rob Roy", which gave the editor a clue as to the sender's identity.'

'Oh, yeah?'

'Yes. I don't s'pose you're much of a reader, Jack?'

'No, I ain't.'

'So, you won't have heard of the novelist, Sir Walter Scott?'

'Nope.'

'Wa'al, he wrote a novel entitled *Rob Roy*, an' it concerned the exploits of a famous Scotch outlaw named Rob Roy MacGregor.'

'So?'

'It seems that, upon receivin' Simon Laidlaw's third or fourth report, the editor suddenly recalled that somebody of the name MacGregor had featured in one of the back numbers of the *Daily News*. It occurred to him that there could be a connection. He had some idea of when the story had appeared in the paper an', therefore, he checked through the back numbers around that time.'

'An' what did he find?'

'He found an article in an inside page about an

accounts clerk stealin' a coupla hundred dollars from his employer an' vamoosin'. The thief's name was John MacGregor, an' he vanished without trace only a few weeks before Scotch John MacGregor carried out his first bank robbery.'

'Gee!'

'The editor concluded that the bank robber was the same John MacGregor who had absconded with his employer's takin's, an' that he'd naturally used the pseudonym "Rob Roy" when contactin' Simon Laidlaw by telegram.'

'You're sayin' that Simon Laidlaw knew Scotch John when he was still livin' in Chicago?'

'I am. The editor didn't know what the connection was between the two of 'em, for he hadn't troubled to find out. Those Scotch John stories had helped sell newspapers an' that was all the damn' editor cared about.' Lansom smiled wryly and continued, 'But I checked up on the pair of 'em an' it appears they are cousins. I also discovered that they had spent some of their childhood vacations with an uncle an' aunt at a horse ranch outside Touchstone, Colorado.'

'You've done well, but where does that git us?'

'It gits us to that other angle I spoke of. Mebbe, instead of searchin' the mountains for Scotch John, you should be lookin' for his cousin. Y'see, I have a sneakin' feelin' that Simon Laidlaw may know the location of the outlaws' mountain hideout.'

'Wa'al, that sure is another angle, one that needs to be explored,' said Stone. 'Yet where am I s'posed to look? If this reporter feller is criss-crossin' the state—'

'Scotch John must have notified him before each robbery where an' when it was due to take place.'

'Yeah, we've already established that.'

'Wa'al, then, Jack, Laidlaw has to have had a permanent base, where Scotch John could get in touch with him each time.'

'You figured out where it is?'

'It has to be somewhere in Colorado, somewhere within an easy ride of all the towns Scotch John has targeted.'

'That makes sense.'

Dave Lansom pulled a well-thumbed map from his inside jacket pocket and spread it open on the table. It was a map of Colorado and the locations of all eleven of the MacGregor gang's crimes were marked with a cross. They formed a rough circle, though the outlaws had not pursued a direct route round it. They had criss-crossed from one point to another. Lansom pointed to the town which lay pretty much in its centre.

'Colorado Springs,' he stated. 'That's where Simon Laidlaw was based, unless I'm much mistaken.'

'I'll head there straightaway,' declared Stone eagerly.

'No,' said Lansom. 'You're too late.'

'Too late?'

'Yeah. You'll find Simon Laidlaw in Touchstone. I'm sure of it.' Lansom grinned and explained, 'I figure he will have reported the story of Fiona Randall's abduction from there. Wa'al, Scotch John has demanded that her father bring the ransom money to Touchstone. Consequently, Laidlaw is bound to stay put, ready to file that story when it breaks. Y'see, Jack, this time there will be no point in his returnin' to Colorado Springs.'

'Guess not. OK, Dave, I'll ride over to Touchstone an' confront the reporter there. I'm sure you're right. That's where he's gotta be,' growled the Kentuckian.

Stone emptied his glass and rose. The two men shook hands and then Stone left the bar-room. Lansom ordered a second beer. He reflected that he had been extremely lucky to encounter the Kentuckian *before* Stone met up with the sheriff.

SEVEN

Dusk had fallen by the time Jack Stone crossed the town limits and rode into Touchstone. Most of the shops and stores had closed, but there were lights showing in the law office, the Last Dime saloon and the Silver Star Hotel. It was to the hitching rail outside the hotel that the Kentuckian tethered his bay gelding. He reckoned that, if Dave Lansom had guessed right and Simon Laidlaw was indeed in Touchstone, the reporter would in all likelihood be residing at the Silver Star.

He entered the hotel lobby and accosted the clerk, who was standing behind the reception desk at the far end.

'Pardon me, but I'm lookin' for a friend of mine,' said Stone.

The clerk looked up and studied the Kentuckian a little warily. The big man's rugged, tough-looking countenance and grim expression did nothing to reassure him.

93

'Er . . . who might that be?' he enquired nervously.

'A feller by the name of Simon Laidlaw,' said Stone.

The clerk brightened.

'Ah, you mean the gentleman who's doin' research for his history of Colorado!' he cried.

'The very same,' said Stone.

'You'll be providin' him with some information, no doubt?' remarked the clerk.

'Somethin' like that,' said Stone.

'Wa'al, Mr Laidlaw is in room number seventeen. Turn right at the head of the stairs.'

'Thank you.'

Jack Stone climbed the stairs and made his way along a narrow passage to the room to which he had been directed. He tapped lightly on the door, but did not bother to wait for a reply. Instead, he straightaway turned the handle and flung open the door. The occupant had removed his hat, jacket, vest and shoes and lay sprawled upon his bed.

'What in blue blazes. . . !' he cried.

'Mr Simon Laidlaw?' enquired the Kentuckian.

'That is my name. And just who the hell are you?'

'Name's Stone. Jack Stone.'

'So, Mr Stone, what do you mean by bursting into my room?'

'I got urgent business that I need to discuss with you.'

'What kind of business?'

'I'm charged by Governor Bill Watson to hunt down an' capture the outlaw Scotch John MacGregor an' his pesky outfit.'

As he listened to Stone's words, Laidlaw stiffened and the colour slowly drained from his cheeks. Yet he determined to bluff it out.

'Well, why are you calling on me? I have nothing to do with any outlaws.'

'No?'

'I'm a historian and I'm here researching—'

'Shuddup!'

'How . . . how dare you tell me to—'

'I said shuddup.' Stone eyed the young reporter with his most ferocious stare. 'I don't want no lies,' he rasped. 'I know that you're doin' here, an' it ain't writin' no history.'

'But I can assure you that I am,' replied Laidlaw quickly, though his voice lacked any real conviction.

Stone laughed harshly and said, 'The editor of the *Chicago Daily News* has revealed that you're the source of the stories, circulatin' in newspapers across the length an' breadth of the United States, 'bout the exploits of Scotch John MacGregor an' his gang.'

'Well, what of it?'

'How'd you manage to turn up at each an' every robbery jest as it happened?'

'I . . . er . . . well . . . er. . . .'

'You turned up 'cause Scotch John telegraphed you, tellin' you where an' when he aimed to strike next.'

'Aw, come on! Are you seriously saying that Scotch John has been detailing his plans in telegrams, which naturally would be read by the telegraphist?'

'I don't suppose he spelled it out that he was gonna carry out a bank raid or a stagecoach hold-up. All he had to do was give you a date an' a place. An' he sure as hell didn't sign the wire as from Scotch John.'

'No?'

'No. Instead, he called hisself "Rob Roy". Am I right?'

Simon Laidlaw gasped. He had not expected Stone to know this. Perspiration beaded his brow.

'What else do you know, or think you know?' he mumbled.

'I know that you're cousins, an' I believe you had a base here in Colorado, where Scotch John knew he could get in touch with you.'

'Indeed?'

'Yup. Colorado Springs?'

Again Simon Laidlaw gasped. His complexion turned a sickly grey and by now he was sweating copiously. He pulled a handkerchief out of his pocket and mopped his forehead.

'We *are* cousins,' he confessed.

'An' you have been usin' Colorado Springs as a base?'

'Yes.' Laidlaw sighed. 'You seem to have it all pretty well worked out,' he said glumly.

'I cain't claim the credit for that,' replied the Kentuckian. 'But, yeah, I do have everythin' pretty much worked out. Scotch John is the same person who fled Chicago six months back with two hundred dollars of his employer's money in his pocket. An' he chose to flee to Colorado 'cause he knew it from childhood holidays spent at his uncle's hoss ranch outside Touchstone. In fact, I reckon the gang's mountain hideout is some place he remembered from back then.'

'I suppose it could be.'

'You shared those holidays.'

'I did.' Laidlaw shrugged his shoulders and murmured, 'I guess we got to know the territory pretty darned well. But I little thought then that one day John would return and use that knowledge to help him pursue a career as an outlaw.'

'He has profited hugely from the many murders an' robberies he an' his accomplices committed.'

'Yes.'

'As you have.'

'Me? No. I swear I've had no share of my cousin's loot'

'You were a junior reporter, a nobody, when Scotch John began his killin's. Now your stories are bein' syndicated in newspapers all over the United

States. You're a made man. An' don't tell me you ain't gittin' well paid for your reports.'

'I don't deny it.'

'The wages of sin.'

'I'm a journalist. It's what I do.'

'But journalists usually only learn about a crime *after* it's been committed. They don't have prior knowledge. I ain't no lawyer, yet I reckon your failure to pass that information on to a peace officer makes you culpable.'

Laidlaw stared uneasily at the Kentuckian. He was no lawyer either, but he suspected that Stone was correct. If the local sheriff were to discover that he had known of his cousin's plans in advance, the lawman would surely clap him straight into jail.

'You guessed that I was using Colorado Springs as a base,' he said. 'So, how come you knew to find me here?'

'That's easy,' replied Stone. 'Scotch John's latest exploit ain't like the others he's pulled. This time he's abducted the daughter of the railway tycoon an' millionaire, James Randall. An', so I'm told, he has demanded a ransom of two hundred thousand dollars, which he's instructed the tycoon to bring to Touchstone. Therefore, if'n you're gonna report on the outcome, it stands to reason you're gonna have to remain here in town. An', since the Silver Star is Touchstone's only hotel, it wasn't too difficult to guess that this is where you'd be stayin'.'

'No, I suppose not.'

'I think this could be Scotch John's last hurrah. What d'you reckon, Mr Laidlaw?'

'Certainly, the ransom money, together with the loot from their various robberies, should be enough to make my cousin and his associates rich men,' admitted the journalist.

'If it is his last hurrah, what will you do?' enquired Stone. 'You'll have no more stories to report back to your newspaper.'

'That's true. But I'll still have my job with the *Chicago Daily News* and, besides, I intend to complete the biography I'm writing.'

'What biography?'

'My cover, while I've been at Colorado Springs, was that I was writing a history of Colorado. Actually, when waiting for my cousin to make his next move, I have been writing, not a history, but rather the definitive biography of Scotch John MacGregor.'

'You think it'll sell?'

'I know it will sell. My reports have made my cousin the most famous outlaw currently roaming the Old West.'

'So, what are you gonna entitle this biography: *The Life and Times of Scotch John MacGregor*?'

'No, though that'll be its subtitle,' said Laidlaw. 'However, I feel that *Portrait of an Outlaw* is a much snappier title. So, that is what it will be. A guaranteed best-seller, believe me.'

'Oh, I believe you!' replied Stone, adding, 'Even when Scotch John has retired from his life of crime, you'll still be profitin' from it.'

'You could put it like that.'

'There ain't no other way to put it.'

'Perhaps not.'

' 'Course, if'n I should hand you over to the local sheriff . . .' Stone left the rest of his sentence unsaid.

But Laidlaw got the drift.

'Look, Mr Stone, I could cut you in for a share of my royalties,' he suggested.

The Kentuckian shot the young journalist a look of utter contempt.

'I ain't about to take no blood money,' he rasped.

'It's not blood money, it's—'

'Shuddup!'

'But—'

'You don't want me to hand you over to the sheriff, right?'

'Er . . . yes . . . right,' mumbled Laidlaw nervously.

'Then you're gonna do exactly what I tell you.'

'And what is that, Mr Stone?'

'That, Mr Laidlaw, is simple. You're gonna take me to Scotch John's mountain hideout.'

'But I don't know where he's hiding out!'

'You admitted that you an' Scotch John spent childhood holidays here in Colorado. At your uncle's hoss ranch.'

'Yes.'

'An' you said that you an' he got to know the territory pretty darned well.'

'Yes, that is so.'

'Wa'al, cain't you think of some remote spot where he's likely to be holed up?'

Laidlaw began to look distinctly shifty and did his best to avoid the other's gaze. 'I . . . I don't know. I . . .' he began.

'Either you come up with a likely hideout or I hand you over to the sheriff. The choice is yours.'

'Well, I'm not sure that—'

'Before I hand you over, I'm gonna beat the hell outa you. 'Deed, you'll probably never walk again. You got two minutes to think about it.'

Laidlaw glanced up. The look on Stone's face told him that the Kentuckian wasn't bluffing.

'OK,' he said. 'I guess I can think of a spot where my cousin might be holed up.'

Instinct told Stone that Laidlaw was being a little less than frank with him. He felt certain that Scotch John had confided in the reporter.

'You know where he's hidin', don't you?' he snarled.

Again Laidlaw dropped his gaze.

'Yeah,' he finally confessed in a low voice. 'I . . . I *do* know where he is lying low. There's an old log cabin, where Uncle Saul used to take us on hunting trips.'

'You'd best guide me to it, then,' said Stone, adding shortly, 'An' don't pretend you cain't find it.'

'No, I can find it. It's situated high up in the mountains, in a small out-of-the-way box canyon, about four miles west of my uncle's old horse ranch and twenty from the Buena Vista ranch, where Fiona Randall was abducted.'

'An' how far from here?'

'Ten or twelve miles, I guess.'

'Then let's git goin'.'

'You promise that, should I do this, you won't hand me over to the law?' said Laidlaw fearfully. 'That you'll let me file my final report and head back to Chicago?'

Stone eyed the reporter contemptuously. Laidlaw could, and should, have prevented several murders and woundings. But he had failed to do so, simply in order to promote his own selfish ends. Well, Stone would give him this promise. However, he felt no compunction about breaking it later.

'OK,' said the Kentuckian. 'You have a deal.'

Laidlaw smiled relievedly.

'I'll need to hire me a horse,' he said.

'Do that an' we'll lam outa town,' said Stone.

At once, Laidlaw proceeded to put on the clothes he had previously discarded. Then, when he was fully dressed, they headed downstairs and out on to the stoop.

Thereupon the Kentuckian unhitched his bay

gelding from the rail outside the hotel, and accompanied the reporter to the livery stables, where Laidlaw hired a mettlesome black stallion.

Touchstone lay in darkness as they rode out across the plains towards the mountains. Even fewer lights spilled out on to Main Street than when Stone had ridden into town. None of the town's shops or stores remained open.

The ride was made in silence, for Simon Laidlaw was feverishly racking his brains to think of some way of eluding the Kentuckian, while Jack Stone was by nature taciturn and, anyway, had nothing he wished to say to the journalist.

It was just before midnight when Laidlaw suddenly reined in his stallion. They had covered several miles of prairie and had reached the foothills of the mountains. Ahead of them loomed a small ranch house, some barns and outbuildings, and a large corral.

'Where are we?' asked Stone, as he pulled up the gelding.

'There is the horse ranch which my uncle once owned. Looks like it's still in use,' said Laidlaw.

'So, why are we stoppin'? You said your cousin an' his gang are holed up some miles west of here, high up in the mountains.'

'That's right.'

'Wa'al, then...?'

'I won't be able to find my way there in the dark.'

103

'There are stars.'

'Even so. We ride through forest and some pretty deep canyons. I believe I can guide you to the hideout during daylight hours. But not now.'

Stone scowled. He was anxious to reach the outlaws' lair and rescue their kidnap victim as soon as possible.

'You sure you cain't find it in the dark?' he growled.

'Yes, I am quite sure,' declared Laidlaw.

'Goddammit!' Stone was half-inclined to disbelieve the reporter and insist that they continue their journey. However, if he were wrong and they did lose their way. . . . He daren't risk it. Glancing round, he observed a stand of cottonwood about thirty yards away to his right. 'OK,' he snapped, 'we ride over into them trees an' dismount.'

Stone was careful to ensure that Laidlaw dismounted first. He had no intention of giving the reporter a chance to ride off.

'Well,' said Laidlaw, 'what now? A few hours' shut-eye?'

'Once I've tied you up,' said Stone.

'Hey, there's no need!' protested Laidlaw.

'There's every need,' retorted Stone.

The Kentuckian produced a length of rawhide from one of his saddle-bags and, without more ado, used it to tie his guide to one of the trees. Laidlaw continued to protest until Stone wearied of his incessant cries and gagged him with some cloth torn from Laidlaw's shirt.

Once Laidlaw was securely fastened to the trunk of the tree, Stone laid out his bedroll and settled down to snatch a few hours' sleep. Laidlaw was not so fortunate. Tied to the tree, he was much too uncomfortable to be able to drop off. An occasional short doze was the best he could muster. For him, the hours passed incredibly slowly.

At last, however, dawn broke and, as the sky lightened, the Kentuckian awoke. Refreshed, he set about preparing breakfast. It was simple enough: beef jerky washed down with coffee. Once Laidlaw had been released and had succeeded in restoring his circulation, he joined Stone at the camp-fire. Both men ate heartily and then, their appetites satisfied, they prepared to depart. Stone extinguished the fire and washed the coffee pot and mugs in a small stream from which he had earlier taken the water he needed. He packed these utensils into his saddle-bags and mounted the gelding.

'OK. Let's go,' he said.

Simon Laidlaw reluctantly mounted his horse. He was still thinking feverishly of some way to escape his captor. He had gone along with the Kentuckian and had agreed to act as his guide solely to avoid being handed over to the law. But perhaps he could lead him into the heart of the wilderness and abandon him there? Surely an opportunity to give him the slip would arise as they traversed the wild, rugged terrain ahead?

'This way,' he said and trotted off westward into the foothills.

Stone followed, though keeping a suspicious eye upon his guide. He knew instinctively that Laidlaw would double-cross him if he could.

They proceeded through the foothills and then began to climb up through thick forest into the mountains. Here and there they emerged from the trees and passed through some ravine or crossed a fast-flowing mountain stream. The four miles from the horse ranch seemed to Jack Stone more like twenty, so steep and tortuous was the route they took. He made a mental note of the various landmarks and changes of direction. In this he was aided by his past experiences as an Army scout. Should the need arise in the future, he had no doubt that he would be able to retrace his steps to the outlaws' hideout.

They came upon it suddenly. Emerging from the forest, they espied beneath them a small hidden box canyon, at the far end of which stood a log cabin and what Stone took to be three small stables. It was hardly surprising, Stone reflected, that the US marshals and other peace officers, who were searching for Scotch John's lair, should have failed to find it.

He noted that there was no smoke curling upwards from the cabin's chimney. Evidently, Scotch John was taking no chances that it might be spotted and had placed himself and his accomplices on iron rations while they remained there. No fresh meat and no coffee were the orders of the day. Unless the searchers stumbled upon the canyon, they would have no inkling that it was there.

Stone assumed that the stables were not being used, for he observed that there were five horses hitched to the rail outside the cabin. When briefing him, the Governor had informed him that Scotch John MacGregor had three confederates. The fifth steed was presumably provided for their kidnap victim.

'OK,' said the Kentuckian, 'dismount!'

'What are you aiming to do?' enquired Laidlaw.

'That ain't none of your business,' rasped Stone. 'Just dismount, will you?'

The ugly glint in Stone's eye warned the reporter that he had better do as he was bidden. Consequently, he slowly, reluctantly, swung himself out of the saddle. He had scarcely reached the ground before Stone leant over and dealt him a swift, vicious blow with the barrel of his Frontier Model Colt. The revolver struck Laidlaw across the top of his scalp and sent him crashing to the ground, where he lay quite still.

Stone also dismounted. He checked to make sure that Laidlaw was unconscious and not feigning, then he took a length of rawhide from his saddle-bag and once again tied the newspaperman to a tree. Then, tearing another strip from Laidlaw's shirt, he gagged him. Next, he hobbled both his bay gelding and the other's black stallion. This done, he was ready to proceed against the outlaws.

Emerging from the edge of the forest, Stone crept forward and peered down into the canyon. The sides were almost sheer, though liberally dotted with scrub. Cautiously, Stone lowered himself over the edge of the canyon and, by hanging on to the various bushes and clumps of brushwood, he succeeded in scrambling down to the canyon floor. This was littered with boulders of all shapes and sizes. Stone chose a particularly large rock and crouched behind it. From this vantage point, he had a clear view of the log cabin, standing no more than twenty yards away.

While he was recovering his breath following his downward scramble, the Kentuckian observed the cabin door open and Limpy Harris appear, framed in the doorway. The outlaw limped out on to the stoop and then crossed to where the five horses stood. He unhitched one of them, a piebald, and slowly swung himself into the saddle. As he did so, Scotch John MacGregor emerged from the cabin. He was wearing his cowboy gear.

'OK, Limpy,' said the red-haired gang chief, 'let's go over it one more time.'

'There ain't no need, boss. I know exactly what I've gotta do,' declared Limpy Harris.

'Nonetheless, we'll run through it once more,' said Scotch John. 'It's important that you git it absolutely right.'

'Wa'al, if'n you say so,' said Limpy Harris, with a resigned shrug of his shoulders.

'Right. Listen carefully.'

'I'm listenin'.'

'You ride into Touchstone an' contact James Randall. I gave instructions he should stay at the Silver Star Hotel.'

'OK, boss.'

'You tell him that the deal is this: he, personally, will bring the two hundred thousand dollars' ransom out here to our hideaway. You will be his guide. Right?'

'Right.'

'An' also tell him that he comes on his own. Apart from you, nobody is to accompany him. An' nobody is to follow him either. Or else. . . .'

'Or else we kill his daughter.'

'You got it, Limpy.'

'I figure Mr Randall will comply.'

'So do I. An' then we'll all be rich.'

'We split the ransom four ways?'

'Of course. That an' the rest of the loot from our earlier robberies. This is to be our swan song. Once we have James Randall's money, we go our separate ways. Me, I guess I'll head for New York, mebbe take me a boat across to the Old Country.'

'England?'

'Scotland. The land of my ancestors.'

Limpy grinned and said, 'Wa'al, I'll make for Frisco. That's one helluva fun city!'

'So I've heard.'

'But what about Mr Randall an' the girl? Do we jest leave 'em here in the cabin'?'

'They'd never find their way back to Touchstone.'

'No.'

'Probably git lost in the mountains an' starve to death.'

'Yeah.'

'It wouldn't be kind to let that happen.' Scotch John smiled wickedly and stated, 'I reckon we had best shoot 'em dead 'fore we leave.'

Harris laughed.

'It sure was mine an' the Duff brothers' lucky day when we recruited you as our boss,' he remarked.

'Yeah, wa'al, we should be long gone 'fore the lawmen back in Touchstone start lookin' for us. They're bound to obey Mr Randall's instructions an' sit tight for a while, awaitin' his an' his daughter's return 'fore takin' any further action.'

'You reckon it'll be some hours 'fore they realize that he an' she ain't comin' back?'

'I do. By then the chances of them catchin' us are gonna be mighty slim.'

Again Harris laughed.

'I'll be on my way,' he said.

'Good luck!' said Scotch John.

From his vantage point behind the large boulder, Jack Stone cursed beneath his breath. He could easily have shot both Scotch John and Limpy Harris, but he dared not. Had he done so, this could have provoked the Duff brothers into killing Fiona Randall.

He continued to observe the outlaw chief. Scotch John, for his part, watched his confederate ride along the canyon floor and disappear into the forest beyond. As he watched, Nick and Dan Duff emerged from the cabin and joined him on the stoop.

Scotch John turned and, producing a cigar case from his vest pocket, offered the brothers a cigar each. They happily accepted his offer. Scotch John then took one himself and returned the case to his vest pocket. Thereupon, he pulled out a packet of lucifers and lit his cigar with one of them, before lighting the others'. They all three stood staring in the direction Limpy Harris had taken, contentedly smoking their cigars.

Stone was tempted to leap out from behind the rock and take them on. However, should he fail to gun down each and every one of them there and then, the survivor, or survivors, could retreat into the cabin and grab the girl as a hostage. He decided, therefore, that he must secure Fiona Randall's safety before tackling the gang.

Once more his time spent as an Army scout

came to his aid. He moved noiselessly, with the speed and agility of a mountain lion. Crawling and crouching, and using the tumble of boulders to screen him from the three outlaws' view, the Kentuckian crept round to the rear of the cabin.

A rear window remained invitingly open. Stone did not hesitate. He grasped the timber sill and heaved himself up and through the window. He landed lightly inside the cabin's main room. This room was sparsely furnished, with a long wooden table in the centre, round which were placed four straight-backed chairs. On one of these sat Fiona Randall, bound yet not gagged. She opened her mouth to speak, but Stone shook his head and placed a finger to his lips. He crossed the room and spoke quietly into the girl's ear.

'The name's Jack Stone,' he whispered. 'An' I'm gonna git you outa here. Jest keep quiet while I set you free.'

He pulled a large double-edged knife from a sheath at his waist. Then he sliced through the girl's bonds. She staggered to her feet and began rubbing her wrists and ankles in an effort to get her circulation going. Stone, meantime, peered out of the front window at the backs of the outlaws, who, quite unaware of what was going on inside the cabin, were still happily puffing on their cigars.

At last, when Fiona had succeeded in restoring the feeling to her limbs, Stone took her by the arm and led her across the cabin to the rear window.

Then, he grasped her by the waist and heaved her through it. He promptly followed.

'What do we do now?' she gasped, once they had both recovered from their exertions.

'Follow me,' said Stone.

He led Fiona back the way he had come. Between the corner of the cabin and the tumble of rocks was a gap of approximately six feet. And it was as the girl crossed this gap that Scotch John chanced to turn round.

'Jesus Christ!' he cried.

Stone turned, grabbed Fiona and pulled her into the cover of the rocks. At the same time, he drew his Frontier Model Colt and loosed off a couple of quick shots. Both struck the nearest outlaw, Dan Duff, in the chest and knocked him flat on his back.

Nick Duff and Scotch John responded, but their shots bounced harmlessly off the boulders behind which the Kentuckian and the girl were hiding.

'Goddammit, that there's Jack Stone!' gasped Nick Duff. 'I saw him one time in Dodge City. He's 'bout the deadliest shot in the West! The man's a livin' legend!'

Scotch John nodded grimly. Although only recently arrived in the West, he too had heard of Jack Stone. While reconnoitring Colorado's townships prior to raiding their banks, he had spent some time in various saloons, where the exploits of the Kentuckian were frequently discussed. After all, Stone was famous for having tamed Colorado's roughest, toughest town, Mallory.

'We're two agin' one,' said Scotch John, as he joined his fellow outlaw, who had dived underneath the stoop, next to where their horses stood hitched.

'So?'

'So, we cain't let him spoil things. Hell, Nick, think about them two hundred thousand dollars we got comin'!'

Nick Duff's face was ashen. He was equal to gunning down some unsuspecting bank clerk or kidnapping a helpless young girl. He was not equal to standing up to a gunfighter of Stone's calibre and renown.

'To hell with the money, I'm gittin' outa here!' he rasped.

'But, Nick—!' began Scotch John.

'Money ain't no use to you when you're dead,' retorted Duff.

He clambered out from his refuge beneath the stoop and fired off a volley of shots in the direction of the rocks behind which Stone and the girl were crouching. Then he hastily unhitched his horse from the rail and climbed into the saddle.

As he did so Stone emerged from behind the screen of boulders and took careful aim. The Frontier Model Colt spat fire and a couple of slugs buried themselves deep in Nick Duff's body. He cried out, yet remained in the saddle. He raised his revolver at the same time as he urged his horse forward. However, before he could squeeze the trigger, Stone fired a third shot.. This struck the outlaw in the centre of his forehead and blasted a mixture of blood, bone and brains out of the back of his skulL Nick Duff was dead before he hit the dirt.

A shaken Scotch John viewed the riderless horse galloping off, while its owner lay motionless on the ground before the stoop. Above him, on the stoop, sprawled the other brother. He, too, was dead, for the second of Stone's slugs had penetrated his black heart.

Nick Duff's panic had transmitted itself to the outlaw chief. No longer was he concerned with his ill-gotten gains. As of that moment, all Scotch John desired was to be gone and out of range of the Kentuckian's deadly gun.

He scrambled out from under the stoop, taking care to keep his steed between himself and the Kentuckian. Swiftly, he unhitched the mare. Then he heaved himself up on to the horse, though making sure that he remained low in the saddle. Indeed, he flattened himself along her back and neck and, digging his heels into her flanks, set the mare galloping off down the canyon.

Jack Stone's sixth shot penetrated Scotch John's Stetson, whistling through his red hair and grazing his scalp. But that was it. Before Stone could reload his revolver, Scotch John, riding furiously, was out of range and heading into the forest beyond.

'Goddammit!' cried Stone. 'The sonofabitch has gotten away!' He turned to Fiona Randall. 'You OK, Miss Randall?' he asked gently.

'Yes.' She looked pale and was still trembling. But, with the departure of Scotch John and the death of the Duff brothers, Fiona was beginning to feel a little less frightened. 'What . . . what do we do now, Mr Stone?' she enquired in a low voice.

'We ride into Touchstone, where I expect your father will be preparin' to accompany Limpy Harris to this hideout,' said Stone.

'What about Scotch John? He's out there some-where,' said Fiona, pointing towards the forest and mountains that lay ahead of them.

'Yeah. But he won't be troublin' us none. He'll be ridin' hell for leather for the state line,' averred Stone.

'I hope so.'

'You can bet on it.' Stone smiled at the girl and said, 'There's somethin' I need to do, 'fore we head towards Touchstone.'

'Oh, yes?'

'Yeah,' said Stone, and he went on to tell Fiona about the part Simon Laidlaw had played, and how he was bound to a tree at the edge of the forest, just above the canyon. 'I gotta release him from that there tree an' take him into town with us,' he explained.

116

'But will he want to come? In the circumstances. . . ?'

'He won't want to,' said Stone. 'Only he ain't gonna have no choice.' And the Kentuckian patted the butt of his Frontier Model Colt.

Fiona smiled.

'I don't suppose he is,' she replied.

EIGHT

Unaware of the fate that had befallen his fellow outlaws, Limpy Harris crossed the town limits, rode into Touchstone and down Main Street towards the Silver Star Hotel. He noted that the law office was situated exactly opposite the hotel. This caused him a momentary twinge of alarm, but he quickly calmed himself. If James Randall wanted to see his daughter alive and well, he would have to guarantee Limpy's immunity from arrest.

Harris reined in his horse and dismounted. He hitched the animal to the rail in front of the hotel and climbed the wooden steps that led up on to the stoop. He entered the building and approached the clerk standing behind the reception desk at the far end of the lobby. The clerk looked up.

'Can I help you, sir?' he enquired.

'You sure can,' said Harris. 'I wanta speak to Mr

James Randall, who, I believe, is stayin' here at your hotel.'

Limpy Harris crossed his fingers as he said this, for, although it was unlikely, it was just possible that the railway magnate had ignored Scotch John's instructions.

'Yessir,' said the clerk. 'Mr Randall is stayin' with us. In our best room.'

The outlaw smiled relievedly.

'Then take me to him. He's expectin' me,' he said.

The clerk had evidently been briefed. He threw Limpy Harris a knowing glance, his jaw tightened and he said coldly and abruptly, 'Follow me.' No 'please' or 'sir', Harris observed.

The room was situated upstairs on the top floor of the two-storey building. The clerk tapped on the door and a voice from inside invited him to enter. It was the largest room in the hotel and the furnishings looked comparatively new. It was uncomfortably full, though, for, besides James Randall and his wife, there were six tough-looking Pinkerton agents present. They were guarding a number of carpetbags, which Harris correctly assumed held the two hundred thousand dollars' ransom money.

James Randall was a tall, dark-haired man, immaculately clad in a grey cravat, a fine cambric shirt, grey silk vest and a well-cut dark-grey frock-coat and trousers. His neat black shoes positively gleamed. Harris observed, however, that the dark hair was greying at the temples and the man's haughty, patrician features were pale and drawn. The strain of the situation in which he found himself had taken its toll.

His wife, Rachel, was a slim, elegant, smartly dressed woman in her early forties. Her chestnut-coloured hair showed no sign of grey, yet her beautiful, finely sculpted face bore a look of anxious melancholy, and her blue eyes looked tired and sorrowful. She, too, was feeling the strain.

James Randall was the first to speak.

'You have my younger daughter?' he said.

The outlaw nodded.

'You ... you haven't hurt her, have you?' enquired Rachel apprehensively.

'Nope. She's OK,' replied Harris. Then he said, 'Mr Whittle, he informed you of Scotch John's demands, I s'pose?'

'Yes,' said Randall.

'He ain't here.'

'No. He has a ranch to run.'

'And my elder daughter has a baby to care for,' added Rachel.

'Yeah. Wa'al, as long as Mr Whittle told you what Scotch John wants in exchange for your daughter's release—'

'Two hundred thousand dollars,' said Randall.

'Yup.'

The railway magnate indicated the pile of

carpetbags that the six Pinkerton men were guarding.

'It's all there,' he said.

'It had better be,' growled Harris.

'Would you care to count it?'

'Nope. Not here, not now. Later, when we make the exchange, then we'll count it.'

'And when and where will that be?' demanded Randall.

'A few hours from now, when we reach Scotch John's hideaway.'

'We?'

'You an' me, Mr Randall. Jest you an' me.'

'No!' cried Rachel. She turned to her husband. 'You can't go alone. How . . . how do we know that this Scotch John MacGregor will keep the promise he gave Jessica and Lloyd and let Fiona go free? He might just take the money and kill you both.'

Limpy Harris suppressed a grin. That was exactly the fate that Scotch John had planned for them.

'Scotch John's a man of his word,' he lied.

'He's a robber and a callous, cold-blooded murderer!' exclaimed Rachel. 'I don't believe he will keep his word!'

'We must pray that he does,' said her husband.

'But—'

'We have no choice in the matter,' said Randall tersely.

'That's right, Mr Randall,' agreed Harris. 'If'n

you fail to comply with Scotch John's demands, your daughter will surely die.'

'We could hold this varmint as a hostage, to ensure your safe return,' suggested one of the Pinkerton men.

'Scotch John don't play those kinda games. 'Sides, how are you gonna find his hideaway without me to act as guide?' enquired Harris.

The Pinkerton man scowled darkly and shrugged his shoulders.

'Dunno,' he muttered.

'So, whaddya say, Mr Randall?' rasped the outlaw.

James Randall glanced at his wife.

'Like I said, I don't believe I have any choice in the matter,' he murmured. Rachel held his gaze, her eyes full of love, tinged with a premonitory fearfulness.

'No, I don't believe you do,' she said quietly. Then, facing Limpy Harris, she raised her voice and stated, 'Take the money and keep your end of the bargain. If you do not I swear I shall have you hunted down, to the ends of the earth if need be.'

Harris dismissed this threat as an empty one. Once the gang had broken up and gone their separate ways, he reckoned there would be little or no chance of their ever being found.

'We'll need a coupla hosses,' he said. 'One for you, Mr Randall, an' for some of them there carpetbags, an' the other to carry the rest of the money.'

'Very well,' said Randall.

'Couldn't perhaps one of your men go with you?' asked Rachel.

Harris shook his head.

'No, Mrs Randall,' he said. 'Your husband won't be needin' no bodyguard.'

'Won't I?' enquired Randall. He rather felt that he might. However, he did not propose to argue the point. 'OK, let's get going,' he said.

'Yeah, let's,' said Harris.

The outlaw led the way out of the room and then downstairs, along the lobby and out into Main Street. James and Rachel Randall followed closely behind, with the Pinkerton agents bringing up the rear and carrying the bags full of banknotes.

By the time one of the Pinkerton men had gone and fetched two horses from the livery stables, Sheriff Joe Norris and Deputy Tim Bannon had emerged from the law office opposite. They crossed the street and the sheriff addressed the railway magnate.

'What's goin' on, Mr Randall?' he demanded.

James Randall jerked a thumb in the direction of Limpy Harris.

'This man here is one of Scotch John MacGregor's gang,' he replied.

Sheriff Joe Norris glared at the outlaw.

'So, what are you proposin', Mr Randall?' he asked. 'Surely you ain't gonna ride out with that no-account varmint?'

'I'm afraid, Sheriff, that I must,' said Randall quietly. He went on to recount the conversation he had had with Limpy Harris and concluded by saying, 'If I'm not back within, say, the next five hours, then come looking.'

'It could take at least six or seven hours for you to git there an' back,' objected Harris.

'OK,' said Randall. 'Make that seven hours.'

Joe Norris grimaced. He guessed that the outlaw was lying, in order to delay the commencement of any search for himself and his confederates for as long as possible. Nevertheless, Norris did not feel that he could say as much. But he determined to wait no longer than a couple of hours before setting out. He wanted to be on the trail of Scotch John MacGregor and his gang as soon after Fiona Randall's release as practicable. Assuming, of course, that Scotch John did actually release her.

'Right, Mr Randall,' said the sheriff. 'If'n you an' your daughter ain't back in Touchstone seven hours from now, I'm comin' lookin' for you.'

'Thank you, Sheriff.' James Randall turned to the Pinkerton agents. 'OK, boys,' he said, 'let's get those bags strapped on to these two horses.'

This was quickly done and, when he was satisfied that the carpetbags were secured, Randall turned and kissed his wife, then swung up into the saddle.

A relieved Limpy Harris mounted his piebald and, leading the second of the two hired horses, headed back along Main Street in the direction of the distant mountains. Randall rode beside him, his face grim and his eyes bleak. He had no illusions that he was taking anything other than a desperate risk. But, if he wanted to see his younger daughter again, he knew it was a risk he must embrace.

The two riders had gone only a couple of hundred yards when, upon passing a buckboard and two accompanying cowboys from the nearby Lazy S ranch, they were confronted by three people crossing the town limits on their way into Touchstone.

Limpy Harris gasped and pulled on the reins of his piebald, bringing it to a sudden halt. He didn't recognize either of the two men, but straightaway he identified the girl as Scotch John's erstwhile prisoner, Fiona Randall.

'Holy cow!' he cried and promptly pulled his revolver from its holster, intending to gun down the two men and attempt to escape with that portion of the ransom money which was strapped to the saddle of the spare horse.

But he never had a chance. Jack Stone immediately recalled Limpy Harris from the short sight he had had of him at Scotch John's hideout. The Kentuckian's Frontier Model Colt cleared leather before the outlaw's gun was halfway out of its holster.

Stone fired twice. Both slugs struck the outlaw in the chest. The first smashed through his ribcage and exited out of his back. The second lodged in his heart and killed him instantly. Limpy Harris was hurled backwards out of the saddle and was dead before he hit the ground.

During the next few minutes half the population of Touchstone seemed to descend upon the scene of the shooting. Rachel Randall was amongst the first to arrive, and she and her husband were quick to help their daughter dismount and then envelop her in their embraces. Stone, meantime, motioned to Simon Laidlaw to dismount.

'Jeeze, what's goin' on here?' exclaimed Sheriff Joe Norris, who, together with Deputy Tim Bannon, had arrived upon the scene at the same time as Rachel Randall. Stone introduced himself and proceeded to relate all that had happened since he had fortuitously met up with the Pinkerton agent, Dave Lansom, in the small cattle town of Castle Rock.

Norris clamped a horny hand upon Simon Laidlaw's arm.

'Guess you're under arrest,' he rasped. Then, turning to the Kentuckian, he said with a grin, 'It sure was lucky you ignored that embargo on goin' after Scotch John an' his gang.'

Stone smiled wryly.

'I ain't inclined to obey orders I disagree with,' he drawled.

'No,' said James Randall, 'you did well. I . . . I was simply afraid that, if I didn't do what the outlaws demanded, they would kill my little girl. But I am glad you saw fit to ignore those instructions to suspend the search.'

'Yes, you saved my life, Mr Stone,' said Fiona. She added softly, 'I do believe Scotch John would have taken the money and killed you and me both, Dad.'

Randall nodded.

'Yes, my love, I daresay you're right.' He smiled at the Kentuckian and remarked, 'We owe you a great debt, Mr Stone.'

'Not jest me,' said Stone deprecatingly. 'Dave Lansom was the one who put me on to this critter, who. . . .'

'Led you to the outlaws' hideout,' cried Simon Laidlaw. 'Without me, you would never have found it.'

'That's true enough,' conceded Stone.

'So, Mr Randall, you've got me to thank, too.' Laidlaw looked imploringly at the railway magnate. 'That being the case, how about asking the sheriff to release me?' he pleaded.

Jack Stone shook his head.

'Oh, no!' he said. 'Don't do that, Mr Randall.'

Laidlaw promptly rounded on Stone.

'You . . . you promised that you wouldn't hand me over to the law if I took you to my cousin!' he exclaimed.

'So I did,' said Stone, 'but I lied. Why in tarnation should you escape justice? Goddammit, if'n you had spoken up at the beginning, you could've prevented Miss Randall's abduction an' also a whole heap of robberies, durin' the course of which several innocent folks were murdered!'

'That's right,' snapped Joe Norris. 'You, Mr Laidlaw, are an accessory before the fact.'

'But . . . but I was only doing my job. I'm a reporter and—'

'Wa'al. You won't be reportin' for some time to come,' said Norris. 'You're gonna spend several years in jail, I promise you.'

'An' by the time you come out, Scotch John MacGregor will no longer be headline news. Any biography you write might sell, but it sure as hell ain't gonna be no bestseller,' declared Stone.

The young journalist's shoulders slumped. He could visualize his future and he didn't like what he saw: a stretch in prison, then failure to find a post on the *Chicago Daily News* or any other newspaper – what journal would employ an ex-jailbird? – and the difficult task of persuading someone to publish his *Portrait of an Outlaw*. His pact with his cousin had turned out to be nothing short of a disaster. He was not about to become a rich man after all.

'What . . . what do you say, Mr Randall?' Laidlaw cried.

'I say that the law must take its course. Lock him

up, Sheriff,' said James Randall.

Laidlaw sighed heavily. He had not really expected the railway magnate to step in and save him. It had been pretty much a forlorn request.

'Take me away,' he said morosely.

Joe Norris turned to his deputy.

'Grab hold of the sonofabitch an' lock him in one of our cells,' he barked.

'Sure thing, Sheriff,' replied Tim Bannon.

The young deputy didn't trouble to handcuff the journalist, but merely grasped him by the arm and marched him along the street towards the law office. Norris, having released his prisoner into his subordinate's custody, smiled at Stone and said, 'Hows about you an' me havin' ourselves a cele-bratory drink?'

'Why not?' said Stone.

'Inform the bartender that the drinks are on me,' stated Randall.

'You won't be joinin' us?' enquired Norris.

'No, Sheriff, for I figure that my wife and I need to spend some little time with our daughter. I'll look into the law office later.'

'Yeah, 'course.'

Randall advised the Pinkerton men that they, too, could enjoy free drinks in the bar-room of the Silver Star Hotel, but said that they should take the carpetbags with them for safe keeping.

'Just make sure you keep that money secure,' he directed.

'You may rely on us, sir,' affirmed the leader of the six.

The main characters in the drama headed back to the hotel, the town's one and only mortician turned up with his assistant, intending to remove the corpse of Limpy Harris, and the crowd, which had gathered at the scene of the shooting, slowly dispersed.

Once inside the Silver Star's bar-room, the Pinkerton men piled up the carpetbags in one corner and seated themselves at the corner table, effectively blocking any passage to the bags. Then two of their number fetched glasses of beer from the bar counter, all supplied at James Randall's expense.

Jack Stone and Joe Norris, on the other hand, remained standing at the bar. But they, too, took advantage of Randall's offer and ordered a couple of whiskeys and a couple of beers.

'Your health, Mr Stone,' declared Norris, raising his glass of beer and quaffing a good measure of the amber liquid.

'An' yours, Sheriff,' said Stone, happily reciprocating.

'So, that's the end of the MacGregor gang,' stated Norris.

'Yeah. Three dead an' one on the run.'

'It's a shame Scotch John got away.'

'He ain't in the clear yet. Once the news of what's happened gits out, every peace officer in

Colorado is gonna be out lookin' for him.'

'Yeah. As soon as I've downed these coupla drinks, I aim to mosey on over to the telegraph office an' send wires to every goddam law office I can think of.'

'You'd best also contact the US marshals' office in Denver.'

'Yup. I'll do jest that.' Norris smiled wryly and growled, 'This here state covers one helluva vast an' rugged territory, an' it sure ain't gonna be easy to search. If only we knew in which direction Scotch John was headin'!'

'You're darned tootin'. He could be headin' west for Frisco, north for Canada, north-east for Chicago, east for. . . . Aw, heck, he could be headin' for jest about anywhere!'

'You ain't got no idea where the sonofabitch is likely to be goin', then?'

The Kentuckian shook his head.

'Nope,' he said. Then he grinned suddenly and added, 'But I know a feller who might.'

NINE

It was mid-afternoon and there were four horses hitched to the rail outside the Wells Fargo staging post at Dingwall's Creek, halfway between the cattle towns of Castle Rock and Touchstone. Jack Stone smiled. He assumed that one of the horses would belong to the Pinkerton agent, Dave Lansom.

As he dismounted and wrapped the reins of his bay gelding round the rail in front of the cabin, Stone surveyed the staging post. It was run by an old-timer named Jerry Beacham and it consisted of the cabin where a traveller might obtain refreshments, a few stables, a small corral and a vegetable patch. Beacham, a widower, lived a simple and mostly lonely existence.

Stone stepped up to the cabin and pushed open the door. The room into which he walked was a bar-room with a fireplace and a few tables at its far end. There was a fire in the grate and two of the tables were occupied. Three itinerant cowboys, returning home at the end of a cattle drive, were hungrily consuming Jerry Beacharn's pork and beans at one table, while sitting at another and enjoying a glass of beer was the slim, elegant, black-clad figure of Dave Lansom. Stone's assumption had proved to be correct.

The Pinkerton man glanced up as Stone came through the door. He raised a welcoming hand. Stone responded, then went over to the bar, where he ordered and paid for a beer. Jerry Beacham watched the Kentuckian as he carried it across the bar-room to join Dave Lansom at his table. The Wells Fargo man observed the two men shake hands. He had heard about Fiona Randall's abduction and subsequent release and how, alone out of the MacGregor gang, Scotch John had escaped into the mountains. He guessed that these two customers were involved in the search for the outlaw, for Lansom's attire indicated to a man of Beacham's experienced eye that he was, in all likelihood, a Pinkerton agent. He wished them well since he would surely feel happier and safer when the murdering miscreant was caught.

'So,' said Stone, as he sat down, 'you got my wire.'

'Yes, indeed,' confirmed Lansom. 'It arrived jest before the sheriff dropped into the Pine Tree Hotel an' informed me that I was free to leave town, an' that the hunt for Scotch John

MacGregor was resumed.'

'That all he told you?'

'He said that Miss Randall had been released and was reunited with her parents.' Lansom gazed curiously at the Kentuckian. 'You wouldn't, by any chance, have had somethin' to do with this turn of events?'

Stone grinned and took a slurp of his beer.

'You were right 'bout Simon Laidlaw knowin' the location of his cousin's hideout,' he said.

'So, you found Laidlaw in Touchstone?'

'I did. At the Silver Star. I persuaded him to take me to Scotch John's lair. It was way up in the mountains, in an extremely remote canyon. Seems the two cousins went huntin' there durin' their childhood.'

'OK. Tell me exactly what happened.'

Stone drank some more beer, then proceeded to relate how he and Laidlaw had ridden up into the mountains and what had happened when he reached the outlaws' hideout.

'So,' he concluded, 'Miss Randall is restored safe an' sound to her ma an' pa, an', with the exception of Scotch John hisself, the MacGregor gang are all dead.'

'Which is why you wired me to meet you here?' said Lansom.

'Yup. I figured we could go after Scotch John together, an' that the quicker we met up the better. If'n that's OK with you, Dave?'

'It's fine with me.' Lansom dug into his coat pocket and produced a slim case of cigars. He offered the case to the Kentuckian and took a cigar himself. Then, when they had both lit up, he said, 'It's a damn' pity that no-account critter got away. But we'll find him.'

'Every peace officer in the state of Colorado is out lookin' for him,' said Stone. 'Only nobody knows where he is headed. Hell, he could hole up in them mountains for months without anyone findin' him!'

'I guess so.'

'Or he could be makin' for the state line. But whereabouts?'

Dave Lansom leant back in his chair and puffed on his cigar. And, as he smoked, he carefully considered the situation. At last he spoke.

'It strikes me,' he drawled, 'that Scotch John must've asked hisself how in tarnation you found his hidin'-place.'

'It could have been a chance find.'

'Sure. But unlikely, tucked away as it is in that remote canyon. So, if I were him, I'd have surmised that someone told you its location. An' there is, as far as I know, only one person who could've betrayed him.'

'Simon Laidlaw.'

'Exactly.'

'So, where does that git us?'

'Wa'al, Jack, I figure that, in Scotch John's

shoes, I'd want revenge. I'd wanta kill the sono-fabitch who had betrayed me. After all, this betrayal has cost him everythin': the ransom he'd hoped to collect from Fiona Randall's father, the loot from the gang's robberies, presumably cached somewhere inside their hideaway, an', of course, his entire gang, all of whom have been wiped out.'

'He didn't know Limpy Harris's fate, but that's a minor quibble,' mused Stone. 'Yeah, I guess Scotch John would dearly wanta avenge hisself. But surely his first thought would've been simply to escape the law?'

'By headin' straight for the state line?'

'Yup.'

'Not necessarily a good idea.'

'No?'

'No, Jack. This is the age of the telegraph. Before Scotch John could cross into another state, Colorado's borders would be under surveillance. Like you said earlier, every peace officer here-abouts would be out lookin' for him. They would-n't know into which state he was headed, but even so. . . . No, his best bet would be to hide out in the mountains until the hue an' cry dies down.'

'Hmm. I guess that makes sense, Dave,' conceded Stone.

'But, before headin' up into the mountains, I reckon he would wanta catch up with his cousin.'

'Wouldn't that be kinda risky?'

'Sure, though not too risky. An' if Scotch John

was mad enough. . . .'

'You b'lieve that's what he's gonna do? Track down an' kill his cousin?'

'I do, Jack.'

'Wa'al, Laidlaw is in jail in Touchstone.'

'Scotch John ain't aware of that.'

'No, I s'pose not.'

'He probably thinks his cousin cut some kinda deal with the authorities, an' that, as a result, he's a free agent.'

'An' is aimin' to make a fortune with that biography he's writin',' growled Stone.

'What biography?' enquired Lansom curiously.

'A biography of Scotch John. He's entitled it *Portrait of an Outlaw*. However, by the time he gits outa jail, Scotch John will be old news. I don't reckon that there biography is gonna earn him so very much.'

'Glad to hear it. Nevertheless, that'll be yet another reason why Scotch John's certain to wanta catch up with his cousin. He sure as hell won't want Laidlaw to live to earn no fortune. No sirree!'

'But how will he find him?'

'When we spoke back in Castle Rock, I said that Simon Laidlaw had to have a permanent base in Colorado, somewhere Scotch John could contact him an' somewhere within an easy ride of all the towns which the MacGregor gang raided.'

'Colorado Springs.'

'Jest so.'

'You think that Scotch John is likely to go lookin' for his cousin in Colorado Springs?'

'I do.'

'But why in blue blazes would he expect to find Laidlaw there?' Stone was clearly sceptical.

Dave Lansom took another puff at his cigaar and then explained, 'Again puttin' myself in Scotch John's shoes,' he said, 'I'd guess that Laidlaw would wanta high-tail it back to Chicago, where he could resume his job at the *Daily News* an' see about gittin' that biography you mentioned published.'

'Yeah,' said Stone. 'That's probably what Scotch John would reckon.'

'In which case, he'd doubtless assume that Laidlaw had left Touchstone an' made for Colorado Springs, where he could board a train bound for Chicago.'

'But, if Laidlaw had done that, surely he would have caught his train to Chicago long before Scotch John could hope to reach Colorado Springs?'

'Mebbe.'

'Mebbe?'

'We know Laidlaw's in jail. However, had he succeeded in cuttin' a deal an' remained a free man, he could easily have acted as I've jest described. Only he might not have boarded the first train outa Colorado Springs.'

'No?'

'No. I figure that, durin' the various periods he's been residin' in Colorado Springs an' awaitin' a summons from Scotch John, he's almost certainly been workin' on that there biography.' Lansom smiled and remarked, 'So, he might be kinda anxious to complete it. That bein' the case, he could easily have delayed his departure from Colorado Springs while he did so. An' that, I put to you, is a possibility which must surely have occurred to Scotch John.'

Stone pondered this proposition. He took a long, deep draught of beer, almost emptying the glass.

'You are sayin' that Scotch John, in his pursuit of Simon Laidlaw, will be faced with two possibilities: either his cousin is already on a train bound for Chicago, or he's sittin' in some hotel room in Colorado Springs, finishin' his manuscript?'

'Yup.'

'An' you figure his thirst for vengeance is enough to persuade him to go lookin' for his cousin in Colorado Springs? Hell, he'd be takin' a mighty big risk!'

'It seems to me that Scotch John is used to takin' risks. An' I'd say he knows that his only chance of exactin' revenge would be to catch up with his cousin there, for there ain't no way he'd git as far as Chicago undetected. Leastways, not for several weeks, mebbe months, when the hunt for him has finally been called off. An' I don't reckon

139

he'd wanta wait that long.'

'OK, Dave. So let's assume he's headin' for Colorado Springs,' said Stone. 'Where does that git us? He's got several hours' lead on us. He will have reached the Springs, searched the town, found Laidlaw ain't there, an' left again 'fore we can git anywhere near.'

'Mebbe, mebbe not. Scotch John cain't take the direct trail. He'd be spotted an' caught for sure. No, he will have to approach the town by a round-about route through the mountains an' forests. Therefore, Jack, if'n we ride hard, we could possibly reach Colorado Springs 'bout the same time he does.'

'We don't know for certain he's headed there,' said Stone.

'No, we don't. It's jest a gut feelin' I've got,' admitted Lansom.

'Hmm. Wa'al, your last gut feelin' worked out pretty well.'

'That was more of an educated deduction.'

'I s'pose it was. But, hell, what have we to lose? Let's assume you're right an' hit the trail.'

So saying, the Kentuckian stubbed out the remains of his cigar and threw back the rest of his beer. The Pinkerton agent promptly followed suit and straightaway they rose from the table.

Jerry Beacham watched them hurry across the bar-room in the direction of the door. He hadn't been able to hear their conversation, yet he surmised what they had been discussing: the whereabouts of Scotch John.

'Good luck, gents!' he called after them.

They paused and turned, and Jack Stone enquired, 'Why d'you think we need good luck? What d'you figure we are aimin' to do?'

'You're out lookin' for Scotch John MacGregor, ain't you?' said the Wells Fargo man.

'We are,' replied Stone, with a grin.

'Wa'al, like I said, good luck!'

Stone and Lansom both smiled and raised a hand in acknowledgement. Then they were gone.

Once outside, the two men unhitched their horses from the rail and quickly mounted. Then they set off at a fair canter. And at the next fork in the trail they took the one that headed southward towards Colorado Springs.

It was early evening of the same day when Scotch John MacGregor rode down from the mountains and on to the trail leading into Colorado Springs. The town was no further than a mile away when he emerged from the scrub.

He was dressed in cowboy's garb, with his wide-brimmed grey Stetson pulled down low, so as to hide his red hair. His jaw was set and his eyes burned with anger. Dave Lansom had divined correctly both the outlaw's feelings and his aims. Scotch John was consumed by his desire for revenge. And he prayed fervently that his quarry

141

remained in town.

Main Street was pretty busy when Scotch John crossed the town limits and headed along it in the direction of the Crystal Queen Hotel. His career as an outlaw had begun there in that hotel. He experienced a sense of *déjà vu* as he approached the Crystal Queen through the early evening traffic. Passengers were disembarking from the stagecoach in front of the stage-line depot; several buckboards were being driven out of town by homesteaders, laden with provisions; citizens, both male and female, were strolling along the sidewalks and popping in and out of the various shops and stores; small groups of cowboys were riding into town and dismounting in front of the town's saloons. Scotch John felt reassured. Surely, in all this hustle and bustle, he would not be recognized?

He dismounted in front of the hotel and wrapped his horse's reins round the hitching rail. Then he clambered up the short flight of wooden steps to the stoop, and there he paused.

Was he on a fool's errand, he asked himself? Was Simon Laidlaw already onboard a train bound for Chicago? The outlaw hoped not. He wanted Laidlaw dead now, not some months in the future. And, once he had taken his revenge, he could concentrate upon his plans for that future. Without Fiona Randall's ransom money, it would not be quite so rosy, yet he would certainly not be

142

destitute. He had resolved what he must do, and it was very little different from the plans he had laid before the abduction had gone so badly wrong.

Scotch John straightened his shoulders and marched boldly into the hotel. A small reception desk stood at the far end of the hotel lobby. A tall, thin, bald-headed clerk presided behind it. Was this the same clerk who had greeted him on his arrival back in April? Scotch John simply couldn't recall. And he prayed that the clerk wouldn't remember him either. Why should he? He must have greeted hundreds more guests in the six months that had passed since Scotch John first set foot in Colorado Springs. Also, on that occasion, Scotch John had not been wearing cowboy gear. He had been dressed as one would expect a typical city gent from Chicago to dress.

As it happened, the clerk did not recognize him.

'Good evenin', sir, how may I help you? Are you lookin' for a room?'

'No. I'm lookin' for a friend of mine,' replied the outlaw.

'Oh, yes?'

'I b'lieve he may be stayin' at this here hotel. He's a historian, who's presently writin' a history of Colorado; how the state came into bein', that kinda thing.'

'Oh, you mean Mr Laidlaw!'

'That's him.'

'He has been usin' us as a base, disappearin'

every so often to conduct his researches, then returnin' here to write 'em up.' The clerk smiled widely and added, 'He's been a good customer, has Mr Laidlaw.'

'If you could tell me which room he. . . ?'

The clerk continued to smile, but shook his head.

'No point,' he said. 'Mr Laidlaw ain't here at the moment.'

'Whaddya mean, at the moment?'

'He went off a few days ago. But he'll be back.'

'Oh, yeah?'

'Certainly, sir. He's doubtless away doin' some historical research, but his gear is still in his room, so I expect him to return shortly.'

'I see.'

Scotch John frowned. It seemed his cousin had not returned from Touchstone. He smiled bleakly. He had no doubt that Laidlaw had betrayed the whereabouts of his hideout to the Kentuckian, Jack Stone. However, he began to think that his cousin had not, after all, cut a deal. Had he done so, he would surely have returned to the Crystal Queen to pick up his belongings, prior to taking a train back to Chicago. So, where the hell was he? Scotch John guessed that he must be in custody, probably in the jail in Touchstone. Consequently, revenge was out of the question. Evading justice was his priority now.

'Do you propose to await Mr Laidlaw's return?'

enquired the clerk.

'No, thanks. I'll catch up with him some other time,' said the outlaw. 'Good day.'

'Good day, sir.'

Scotch John turned and retreated back down the lobby. He pushed open the front door and stepped out on to the stoop. Then he clattered down the steps to the street and unhitched his horse.

It was as he was in the process of mounting that he observed, among the horses and riders and the buckboards and gigs passing up and down Main Street, two horsemen approaching, one of whom he recognized. The man was too far off for Scotch John properly to distinguish his features, but his build, the way he held himself, and the buckskin jacket he wore were enough for the outlaw to identify the famous Kentuckian gunfighter who had shot the Duff brothers.

Straightaway, Scotch John wheeled his horse round and set off at a gallop along Main Street, in the opposite direction. By the time Jack Stone and Dave Lansom reined in their steeds in front of the hotel, the outlaw had disappeared from view and was fast approaching the edge of the town. Due to the other traffic proceeding up and down Main Street, neither man had spotted their quarry.

'Let's start here,' said Lansom. 'As Colorado Springs' only hotel, it's gotta be here where Simon Laidlaw made his base.'

'I guess so,' agreed Stone.

The two men quickly dismounted and hitched their horses to the rail outside the hotel. Then they hurried up the steps on to the stoop and into the hotel lobby.

The tall, bald-headed clerk looked up from behind his desk. It was proving to be a busy evening.

'Howdy, gents,' he greeted the Kentuckian and the Pinkerton agent.

'Howdy,' said Stone. 'We're lookin' for a friend of ours, who we b'lieve is stayin' at this here hotel.'

'Indeed?' The clerk quietly studied both men for a moment or two before asking, 'Your friend wouldn't, by any chance, be Mr Laidlaw the historian?'

Stone and Lansom exchanged glances.

'That's the feller,' said Stone. 'How'd you guess?'

' 'Cause you ain't the first person to ask after Mr Laidlaw,' explained the clerk.

'No?'

'No. Another friend of his was askin' after him only a few minutes ago. You have jest missed him.' The clerk smiled and added, 'As I told him, Mr Laidlaw ain't here at the moment. Off pursuin' his historical researches, I expect.'

'Yeah.' Stone immediately guessed that Laidlaw had assumed the guise of an historian to explain his sudden departures from the Crystal Queen.

But that was of little or no interest. What did interest him was the fact that Laidlaw had had someone else enquiring after him. Surely it had to be their quarry?

'This other friend, what was he like?'

The clerk shrugged his shoulders.

' 'Bout medium height. In his mid-to-late twenties, I'd say. An' dressed in cowboy gear.'

'Did you recognize him?'

'No. But then, there are several ranches nearby an' I sure as hell don't know all the cowpokes around here. I mean, these fellers come an' go.' The clerk then had a sudden recollection. 'One unusual thing, though,' he said. 'Somebody had shot a bullet clean through the feller's Stetson. Both bullet holes were plain to see. Me, I'd've bought another hat.'

'Thanks, you've been most helpful,' said Stone.

As he and Lansom turned to leave, the clerk called after them, 'You wanta leave a message for Mr Laidlaw?'

'No,' replied Stone. 'I don't reckon so.'

Outside on the stoop, the two men halted and peered anxiously up and down Main Street.

'So, we missed the sonofabitch by a mere matter of minutes,' sighed Lansom.

'Yeah, goddammit!' growled Stone.

'Which way did he go? That's the question.'

'An' where's he headed? You got any ideas?'

'Too many.'

147

'Hmm. Me, too.'

Dave Lansom had earlier succeeded in putting himself in Scotch John's shoes and, by so doing, tracking him to his cousin's base in Colorado Springs. But could either he or Jack Stone do the same a second time?

TEN

Scotch John MacGregor, having ridden through the night, reined in his weary horse outside a small, lonely way station midway between his mountain fastness and the town of Touchstone. He, too, was weary and, in addition, ravenously hungry. But he could afford to take no chances. Consequently, as he approached the way station, he had scanned it and its environs to ensure that he was its only visitor. Satisfied that this was the case, he dismounted and entered the building.

A few minutes later he was tucking into a hearty breakfast of thick-cut cornbread, pork and beans, while the station's manager, a short, bandy-legged half-breed, attended to his horse, watering and feeding the exhausted animal.

Scotch John slowly digested his meal and, at the same time, carefully considered his position. His urge for revenge had evaporated. What he must do now was avoid capture. He went over in his head what he had earlier planned to do.

A quick dash for either the Utah or the Nebraska border was out of the question. The chance of his being spotted by some of the many peace officers out looking for him was all too likely.

In any event, it was the eastern seaboard that he wanted to reach. But that would entail a very long journey, and it was almost certain he would be detected and arrested before he could complete it.

His best option was to hide out in the mountains until, eventually, the forces of law and order gave up the hunt. However, that would take several weeks, even months, and winter was fast approaching. He could not survive a winter in the mountains without some form of habitation, a log cabin or, at the very least, a tepee.

Scotch John smiled to himself. Those out searching for him would, he felt sure, be expecting him to head for, and cross somewhere along, the state line. The last place they would dream of finding him had to be his old hideaway. That being so, the outlaw determined to wait out the winter there.

He finished his breakfast and, having lit a cigar, lingered over his coffee. He was anxious to be on his way, yet knew that he had to allow his horse a short rest. The beast was close to exhaustion and the outlaw had several miles of mountain terrain to cover before he reached the hidden box canyon. He could not afford to have the horse collapse under him.

Presently, feeling that he should delay no longer, Scotch John rose from the table. He extinguished the butt of his cigar beneath his heel and headed towards the door. As he approached it, it swung open to reveal the half-breed and another man.

The newcomer was none other than Deputy Tim Bannon from Touchstone. The sheriff had formed a posse and had dispersed its members in ones and twos to search the foothills north of the town. Bannon had ridden alone and had ventured further into the mountains than any of the others. However, he had discovered no trace of his quarry and now was on his way back to Touchstone. But, like Scotch John, he had experienced severe pangs of hunger and, upon spotting the way station, had decided to break his journey there and get something to eat.

Scotch John had already settled accounts with the half-breed and so he promptly said, with a smile, 'Thanks. That was a darned good breakfast.'

'Wait a minute.'

Tim Bannon's words caused Scotch John to pause and glance in the deputy's direction. Their eyes met. There was a hint of recognition in the lawman's eyes.

'I'm kinda in a hurry,' said Scotch John.

'Don't I know you from somewhere?' enquired the deputy.

151

'I don't think so, for I sure as hell don't know you,' retorted Scotch John.

Nor did he. But the thought occurred to him that perhaps the deputy had seen him all those years ago, when he and Simon Laidlaw visited their uncle at his horse ranch. Certainly, he had changed since then, yet it was possible that there was something in the man that reminded the deputy of the boy.

'There's somethin' 'bout you that's familiar,' mused Bannon.

'Wa'al, I used to visit an uncle in these parts some years back,' said Scotch John, thanking his lucky stars he was wearing his cowboy garb and not the city-style clothes, which he had invariably worn when robbing banks or holding up stagecoaches.

He had observed the deputy's badge and guessed that Bannon was out looking for him. But there was no good reason why the deputy should suspect him. He was not, after all, riding hell for leather for the state line.

'You don't live in these parts no more?' said Bannon.

'Nope. I'm headin' up into Wyomin'. A friend's got a ranch there. Asked me to join him.'

'I see. You didn't, by any chance, notice a lone rider on your travels? He'd likely be wearin' a dark grey suit an' a derby hat.'

'No, cain't say I have.' Scotch John had been tempted to say 'Yes' and send the deputy off on a wild-goose chase. But he had resisted the urge, figuring that, should he do so, Bannon might later realize he had been lied to and, consequently, direct other searchers to that region. 'Who are you lookin' for, Deppity?' he asked.

'Scotch John MacGregor. You've heard of him?'

'I'll say.' Scotch John whistled. 'Good luck to you,' he remarked and made to push past Bannon and the half-breed, both of whom were still standing in the doorway.

' 'Fore you leave,' said Bannon, 'would you kindly remove your hat?'

Scotch John halted in mid-stride and stepped back a couple of paces.

'An' jest why would I do that?' he enquired.

'I wanta see the colour of your hair,' replied Bannon. 'Y'see, if'n it's red—'

He got no further. Realizing that the game was up, Scotch John went for his gun. The Colt Peacemaker came out of his holster in one swift, continuous movement. Bannon's Remington had barely cleared leather when the outlaw's first shot hit him in the chest and sent him tumbling backwards through the open doorway. Scotch John's second shot ripped into the centre of the half-breed's forehead and blasted his brains out of the back of his skull. Both men sprawled in a heap outside the way station.

Still clutching his revolver, Scotch John walked slowly across the cabin floor towards the doorway.

He kept the gun levelled at the two motionless bodies, not certain whether they were quite dead.

However, he need not have bothered. Both were dead, Scotch John's first bullet having penetrated Deputy Tim Bannon's heart and killed him instantly.

The outlaw was now faced with a dilemma. Sooner or later, the bodies of the deputy and the half-breed were sure to be discovered. And, when they were, an intensive search of the area would begin. In these circumstances, it was all too likely that the searchers would enlist Simon Laidlaw, whom he was now convinced lay incarcerated in Touchstone's jail, to lead them to his hideout. He determined, therefore, to stop at the hideout only long enough to pick up some provisions and the loot, which he had hidden there. Then he would head on deeper into the mountains, where surely he could find a cave in which to spend the winter months until such time as he judged the hunt for him had been abandoned.

Scotch John smiled grimly as he ran his eye over Bannon's horse, hitched to the rail outside the cabin. This was just what he needed: a fresh horse. Abandoning his exhausted steed, he unhitched Bannon's piebald mare and quickly mounted her. Then he turned her head and resumed his journey onward and upward into the mountains.

The ride took him through stretches of dense forest, across several tumbling mountain streams and patches of slithering scree, and into and out of various deep and gloomy ravines. Indeed, such was the tortuous trail he took and the rugged terrain he was forced to traverse, that it was past noon before the outlaw eventually reached the edge of the forest immediately above the small well-hidden box canyon.

He peered down into it. Apart from a lone coyote slinking in and out of a tumble of rocks, the canyon was deserted. Scotch John carefully scanned the log cabin and the three small stables. There was no smoke spiralling upwards from the cabin's chimney and no sign of life.

Satisfied, the outlaw made his way down the side of the mountain and through the trees to the mouth of the canyon. He entered it and trotted slowly up its length towards the cabin. Then, upon reaching the cabin, he dismounted and tied the mare to the hitching-rail.

It was as he ducked under the rail that the front door of the cabin suddenly opened and two men stepped outside, the same two whom he had seen on the previous evening, approaching Colorado Springs' Crystal Queen Hotel.

'Afternoon, Mr MacGregor,' said the taller and bigger of the two.

'Jesus Christ!' Scotch John stared flabbergasted at the two men confronting him.

'He ain't gonna help you,' said Stone.

'He sure ain't,' added Dave Lansom.

'How ... how. . . ?' Scotch John was lost for words.

'Surprised to see us, huh?' said Stone. He smiled grimly and remarked, 'We almost met here a day or two back, only you left in one helluva hurry, 'fore I could introduce myself.'

'I . . . I know who you are. You're Jack Stone, the famous Kentuckian gunfighter,' gasped Scotch John.

'An' this here's Mr Dave Lansom, a Pinkerton agent engaged by the Cattlemen's Bank to hunt you down.' Stone continued to smile grimly. 'Wa'al, I reckon he's done jest that,' he added.

'You . . . you figured I'd head back here?' stammered Scotch John.

'It wasn't too difficult,' said Lansom. 'Where else would you go?'

'I could've aimed to cross the state line, either north, south, east or west.'

'Yeah, that was possible. But with every lawman in the state out lookin' for you, I didn't think so. It seemed more likely you'd head back up into the mountains.'

'An', with winter comin', you'd need shelter an' provisions, both of which you knew you could find here,' stated Stone.

'I see.'

'Also, there was all that loot you'd accumulated over the last six months,' growled the Kentuckian.

'Yeah, ironic ain't it?' said Lansom. 'Instead of

havin' to split it four ways, now that the rest of your gang are dead, it's all yours. That must about make up for the loss of the ransom you were hopin' to collect from James Randall.'

Scotch John glowered at the Pinkerton agent.

'Did you find it?' he asked.

'Sure we did.' Lansom jerked his thumb over his shoulder towards the cabin. 'In there, beneath the floorboards.'

'A small fortune,' said Stone.

Scotch John eyed the two men speculatively. He was not beaten yet.

'Whaddya say we divide it three ways?' he enquired.

Jack Stone and Dave Lansom exchanged glances.

'You gotta be jokin',' said the Kentuckian.

'Why? Nobody'd ever know. You let me go with one third of it, an' take the rest. Hell, this is your chance to make some real money!' cried the outlaw.

'I don't want no blood money,' retorted Stone.

'Me neither,' said Lansom.

'You mean. . . .'

'We mean, we're takin' you in an' handin' over the proceeds of your robberies to the authorities to sort out,' said Stone.

Scotch John studied the faces of the two men. They stared back at him, their expressions grim and implacable. The prospect of sharing his ill-gotten gains evidently held no attraction for either man. They were determined to take him back to Touchstone, where he would stand trial for his crimes. And he knew that there could be only one outcome of such a trial. He would be found guilty and he would hang.

The courage, which had deserted Scotch John during Jack Stone's earlier visit to the box canyon, slowly returned. On that occasion, Nick Duff's panic had communicated itself to him. He, too, had then panicked and had fled. But this time flight was out of the question. Scotch John could either meekly surrender or stand and fight.

'You want me, you're gonna have to take me,' he snarled.

'I don't reckon that'll be a problem,' drawled Stone.

'Wa'al, you're two against one,' said the outlaw. 'That ain't right. You gotta give me a fair chance.'

'Jest like the chance you gave your defenceless victims?' rasped Stone.

'Aw, to hell with it! You take him, Jack,' said Lansom, and he slowly pulled the .30-calibre long-barrelled Colt from the shoulder rig beneath his frock-coat and laid it down on the stoop. Then he stepped a few paces to his left.

'OK,' said Stone. He faced the outlaw and stated flatly, 'It's your call.'

Scotch John realized that this was the moment of truth. His career as a Western outlaw had begun with his gunning down, amongst others, the marshal at Colorado Springs, and, only a few hours earlier, he had outdrawn yet another lawman. Two professional gunfighters, and he had killed both of them. So what if Jack Stone did have a fearsome reputation? Perhaps it was exaggerated?

The outlaw dropped his hand on to the butt of his Colt Peacemaker and whipped it clean out of its holster in one swift move. But he was not quick enough. Before he could aim and fire the gun, Stone's revolver spat fire and a .45-calibre slug struck Scotch John in the right shoulder, ripping through his body and exiting out of his back in a stream of blood and splintered bone. Scotch John screamed and, as the force of the shot sent him sprawling on to his back, his gun slipped from his nerveless fingers.

Stone stepped forward and retrieved the discarded weapon.

'Usually, I shoot to kill,' he drawled. 'But, I sure as hell didn't want you to escape that hangin' you so richly deserve.'

Scotch John groaned. Then, as the pain subsided a little, he sank inexorably into a pit of black despair.

It took Jack Stone and Dave Lansom only a few minutes to bring their horses from the stables, where they had hidden them. Then they set to packing their saddle-bags with the banknotes they had found inside the cabin. Those which they couldn't fit into the saddle-bags they packed into a couple of carpetbags that they had also found in the cabin. And, once they had secured these bags to their saddles, they turned their attention to the outlaw.

Using strips torn from Scotch John's shirt, Stone stanched the flow of blood and bandaged the outlaw's shoulder. Then he tied the outlaw's wrists together with whipcord and, aided by Lansom, lifted him up into the saddle.

Thereupon, the Kentuckian and the Pinkerton man quickly mounted their horses and, flanking Scotch John MacGregor, set off down the canyon and into the forest. For Scotch John, it was going to be a most unpleasant and painful ride, yet he was in no hurry to complete it. He knew what awaited him in Touchstone, namely a trial and then, inevitably, the gallows.